Trouble In Beer City

A Ricky Temple PI Story

Book 1

by Joe Quigley

First paperback and digital editions published in 2024
by Kindle Direct Publishing

This story is set in Asheville, North Carolina and was written prior to
destruction caused by Hurricane Helene. It is in no way intended to make
light of the situation affecting my hometown.

This is a work of fiction. Although a few characters are based on friends
of the author, the majority are from the author's imagination just like the
story itself. Some locations are real, some location names were slightly
changed for fun.
It's entertainment.

Cover design and formatting by Amy J. West
with resources from Joe Quigley, Canva.com, istockphoto.com, and
Flaticon.com

Contact joequigleyauthor@yahoo.com for further information.

Paperback ISBN 979-8-218-55904-5

This book is dedicated to my wife April who endured reading many versions. Her inspiration and support helped me get to this point.

A special thanks to my parents, for everything over the years.

Also, to the individuals who inspired the characters RJ Floyd, Susan Temple, and Father Tim Daniels, thank you. All three of you have been an important part of my life.

A special thanks to Warren Haynes and Gov't Mule for the song "Endless Parade."

Contents

Chapter 1

"Are you scared of rats or something? Stop watching the rats and pick the lock. We need to get inside before someone sees us. I thought you watched a video online to learn to do this," Jimmy yelled at Billy adding more pressure he didn't need. "We need to be in and out in thirty seconds." Lucky for them, the door they were trying to pick was on the backside of the building and the overhead light was conveniently out.

"The video had a different kind of lock," Billy said, trying to defend himself while he kept an eye on the rats running across his feet at the same time. He finally popped the lock at the back entrance of Circus Act Brewery and the two ran inside and pulled all the tap handles forward, allowing the beer to flow out. Within a few seconds they were back outside and walking, at a normal pace, to where they parked the car.

"Losing all that beer will hit their pockets for sure," Billy said as they drove the few blocks to the Asheville Beer Facility to do the same thing. Originally, they wanted to hit three breweries tonight but decided not to push their luck. Opening the door went smoother this time since Jimmy brought a crowbar and pried it open instead of waiting on Billy. After opening all the taps at the second brewery, they left and drove a roundabout way back to Billy's house where the others were waiting.

Ronnie Jenkins, Jimmy O'Brien, Dave Finley, and Billy Thompson were sitting in Billy's basement, listening to Jimmy and Billy tell the story of their adventure. They were known as "the Boys," a name they had been called since either kindergarten or first grade. Nobody really knew how it started, but it was debated often. One story was their kindergarten teacher called them that because they were inseparable. Another story was they gave the nickname to themselves. Either way they've shared every major life event together and probably will forever. All but Billy had graduated from Western Carolina University eight years ago and came back home to Asheville expecting to find the same town they had left. They were wrong.

Billy didn't really care that he'd never graduated from college. He was making a good life for himself working for a West Asheville pool company. He worked hard over the years and was being rewarded for his effort. He was a short stocky guy who had the classic mountain guy look: beard, green trucker hat and strong, the kind of strength that comes from working with your hands.

Ronnie, the unofficial leader of the group, is the branch manager for a bank downtown where he started as a loan officer and worked his way up over the years. He has a certain charisma, and he looks like a banker. A slim build, short but not too short hair, and could pull off a suit, business casual, or a relaxed look in jeans and a knit shirt. Truth be told, he was usually in shorts, flipflops and a t-shirt. His shadow beard still looked professional and went well with his relaxed, easy-going demeanor that works in the business world or when he chats up girls in a bar. He has confidence about him, and you know when he is in the room.

Jimmy and Dave had always been very close, so it surprised no one when they announced on graduation day they were going into business together. Their new landscape business would be called Cats Landscaping. After being told that it was the dumbest name for a landscaping company, they dug in, and the name stuck. Jimmy and Dave loved to be outside, and they knew from the beginning their hard work would overcome a bad name. Jimmy had that outdoor look. He always had his sunglasses on, some sort of hat, and is very skinny, some would say scrawny. Jimmy was always on the go and liked it that way. But Dave was more like Billy. He enjoyed his beer and had that brute strength that comes with working with your hands.

They were family: they looked out for each other.

Asheville had changed from the quiet mountain town of the seventies and eighties that was mainly known for the George Vanderbilt Biltmore Estate to a microbrew mecca. Add in the Blue Ridge Parkway with its scenic views, hiking, rafting, low humidity in the summer, and most importantly a new city marketing campaign, and you have a massive increase in tourists. The out of towners decided they wanted to be residents, and over a 10-year span the small mountain town saw a large influx from around the country.
Real estate and the cost of living was cheaper, so the new residents moved in with bulging wallets and drastically changed the Asheville economy. The Boys hated it.

They decided they were ready to bring Asheville back to the way it was when they and generations of their families had grown up. They felt the town was a better place when you could drive through downtown without dodging the hippies and tourists. Not to mention the friendliness of waving to people, even if you didn't know them. It was a comfortable place to live, but when Dave's parents were turned down for a mortgage, it was the last straw, and the Boys decided it was time to act. It started with organizing a quiet boycott – no publicity -- among locals who felt the same way they did. The boys felt they were easy targets. When the boycott was taking too long, they escalated to other money draining techniques. With Ronnie's leadership and inside help, they had avoided being identified as the leaders. Nobody had been caught or even questioned.

Clif Jordan unlocked the front door of Circus Act Brewery, walked in, and locked the door behind him. As the owner he is always the first to arrive each day. Walking toward the bar, he realized he was standing in a puddle of beer. He looked behind the bar to see all his beer handles pulled and his beer all over the floor. Clif also noticed sunlight coming in from the back door. He walked to the back of the building to find the door open so he grabbed a cloth to pull it shut, careful not to disturb any evidence the police would need to find out who had broken in. After Clif closed the back door, he turned to look at his tap room. He stared for several seconds before getting to work and assessing the damage. When he was done, his first call was to the police and his second was to his friends who owned a couple of the other breweries.

"They got me too," Mike Lamb said. Mike owns the Asheville Beer Facility a few blocks away. "I called Brian Johnson over at Coxe Ave Brewery already. He was spared," Mike told his friend. "I'm going to close for the day and get cleaned up and check my inventory to see what I have ready so I can open tomorrow."

"Same here. Let's meet up this afternoon at Brian's place and talk," Clif said.

Father Tim Daniels walked around downtown Asheville as he often does when his duties allow. He likes to visit with local business owners to get a feel for the city. He was from Asheville but had moved away a few times over the years. When he was ordained, he asked to be sent to the mountains of Western North Carolina. Now he has a small Parrish just outside the city. He feels as though this is his city.

He walked into Coxe Ave Brewery and was surprised to see so few people. Although it was early in the week, it was leaf peeping season in the Great Smoky Mountains so there were usually tourists everywhere. As he entered, he noticed Brian Johnson, the owner, sitting at a table with Clif Jordan and Mike Lamb.

"I see how it is Father Tim, going to one of my competitors now," Clif Jordan said laughing.

"You guys know I frequent all three of your breweries equally," he laughed as he walked over to the table with the three owners. "How are things going?"

"Clif and Mike are closed today. Last night someone broke in and opened all their taps to drain their beer. We are meeting to talk about our options," Brian said, returning from the bar as he got Father Tim his favorite stout.

"Any other damage or anything stolen?" Father Tim asked.

"No. All they did was open the taps. It will be a hit on our bottom line because of the cleanup, having to close today, and replacing the beer we lost. The good thing is we have enough beer already kegged so we will both be able to open tomorrow. To make up for the beer we lost I already have the head brewer running batches, but it won't be ready until next month. If we are lucky, we will be able to pace out our inventory enough to stay open," Clif said. Mike nodded in agreement.

"We called in a cleaning crew so the brewers could be free to start new batches. But like I said, that's even more money out the door," Mike added.

"Any idea what's going on or who might have an issue with you guys?" Father Tim asked.

"No. To make it worse, we've also had a decrease in business over the last couple of months. We still get the tourists, but the locals don't come in as much. We need their business during the winter months. I try to keep all of this out of the media, but you know how WAVL is. They report with or without facts," Clif explained.

"Which is why we are here today," Brian said. "We are talking about hiring someone to figure this out and put an end to it. You know my brewery is the newest one so I really can't afford too much of this, but the three of us work together where we can. It really helps. Like the warehouse we share, that helps me in several ways."

"Do you have someone in mind to hire?"

"Not yet. Do you know someone?" Clif asked.

"I do. He grew up here then went to college at Western Carolina University, so he is a local guy who knows Asheville. He hasn't lived here in a long time, so not a lot of the newer residents will recognize him. He joined the military and put in his twenty years. Once he retired, he started a private investigator business over in High Point and has a house out on the Outer Banks where he and his wife spend a lot of time. While in the military he did some special operations stuff and worked at The Command. I am a little biased because we grew up together, but I trust him. His name is Ricky Temple."

Father Tim took a sip of his stout, realizing he had taken over their meeting. He was just trying to help. He excused himself from the table to give the business owners a chance to talk and went to the bar to finish his beer. As he finished, he asked the bartender for his bill.

"Sorry boss, no bill for you. Brian said your dinero is no good here," Harvey the daytime bartender said.

Father Tim thanked Harvey and shot a wave to Brian as he walked to the door. Before he got there, Clif Jordan stopped him. "Can you give me this Ricky guy's phone number? Your word on him is good with us."

"Of course, tell him I told you to call. Trust me, you need Ricky T."

Chapter 2

Standing on the beach, listening to the rhythmic crashing of the waves is one of life's simple pleasures for Ricky Temple. For some reason it's even better on the Outer Banks. He could never put his finger on why, it was just different. The Outer Banks, the 200-mile line of barrier islands off the coast of North Carolina, reaches from the Virginia border to midway down the North Carolina coast. The islands are accessible by ferry boat or a series of bridges and are divided into the southern and northern beaches. The southern islands are quiet and remote with plenty of beach houses on the Atlantic Ocean and the Sound for quiet family vacations. The northern beaches are more commercialized and congested but have a definitive charm that other beach towns simply don't have. Here in Kill Devil Hills, Ricky and Susan Temple bought their beach house.

Ricky turned from watching a shrimp boat at just the right moment to see one of his favorite sights, his wife returning from her morning walk. Susan's strawberry blonde hair was blowing in the wind coming off the water, which was stronger today than it had been lately. Ricky has always loved that smile of hers, it was infectious. They were friends in college and reconnected about 10 years ago. After chatting online for a few months, they decided to give their relationship a shot and see what happened. It worked. At the time Ricky was still in the military and Susan was working in Boston, so they managed a long-distance relationship for a couple of years. Ricky spent a lot of time on airplanes, and he came to love everything about the city, especially their sport teams. He knew the small town he lived in outside base wasn't as exciting as the big city, so he didn't push Susan to travel to North Carolina early in the relationship.

When the time came for Ricky to retire from the military, he and Susan had a long talk about what they wanted to do in the next phase of their work lives. One thing they agreed on was they wanted to enjoy life, so Ricky and Susan decided on new careers.

Ricky got his private investigator license. Susan has a master's degree in museum studies from Harvard and worked in museums assisting curators with artifact processing and research. No matter where they moved, there was always a museum that needed her skill. Using her years of experience, she started her own business offering her skills on a contract basis. When a museum received a large artifact donation, they could contract with Susan to assist with the cataloging and research. It meant she had to travel some, but Susan and Ricky loved to travel. Now they both had jobs where they could control their schedules.

As Susan got closer to him, he could see the expression on her face that he knew well. He knew what was coming next.

"I'm hungry and my hair looks like shit from the wind," Susan said. "How about we stop at The Front Porch Café on the way home to get coffee and a snack?"

"You sure you don't want to go to the Jolly Roger for breakfast? It's not that far," Ricky suggested. He already knew the response.

"No, let's just get coffee and a snack," she said, as she turned toward the parking lot.

"Ok, that sounds good. Shall we go?" Ricky asked, extending his arm to her.

"We shall," Susan said with a laugh as she took his arm and the two of them walked towards the car.

It was still warm, but you could feel fall wasn't far off from the Outer Banks. The wind and water were already getting cooler and there were fewer people around. As they entered the parking lot, they brushed as much sand as they could off their feet. Susan put on her flip flops and Ricky put on his Birkenstocks. As they reached their blue BMW X3, Ricky opened the door for Susan who sat on the edge of the seat. As she always did when they went to the beach, Susan had a bottle of water and a towel in the front seat to finish cleaning her feet. Ricky did the same. Susan passed the bottle of water now with only a quarter remaining and he grabbed the wet towel to "dry" off his feet and then got in and closed the door.

Ricky adjusted his Red Sox hat and saw it was 9:00 as they pulled out of the parking lot and onto the beach road. He worked his way to the main highway for the short drive to their favorite coffee shop. It was a popular place even in the off-season, so it was crowded.

After Ricky parked, he got out of the car and walked around to open the door for Susan. As they walked toward the door Ricky felt his phone vibrate. He looked at the number and put the phone back in his pocket. After many years of being attached to his phone and being on a strict recall status in the military, Ricky decided when he retired, he would turn his ringer off and only answer his phone if it was someone he knew. He learned the combination of not answering his phone and not watching the news made his life much more peaceful.

"Who is it?" asked Susan.

"No idea, it looks like an Asheville number. You know my rule. If a name doesn't show on caller ID and they don't leave a message, then I probably don't need to talk to them," Ricky replied.

"Yes dear. Do you want your usual?" Susan asked.

"Sounds good, and since we are heading home in a few days, let's look at some mugs and coffee to bring with us. We always forget to bring mugs back to the condo in High Point."

Ricky saw that nobody was sitting at their favorite table, so he walked over and put his Red Sox hat on it to claim it. He liked to have a table towards the back of the coffee shop with a seat facing the front door, another trait from his previous life. Susan went to the counter and got the usual order: one large black coffee, a cinnamon roll, a small latte with oat milk, and a chocolate-filled croissant. Today she added a couple of pound bags of coffee and two Front Porch Café coffee mugs. After getting their order from the counter she joined Ricky at the table.

As Susan sat down, she asked, "Do you have any cases to get home to?"

"No. Nothing. Have you heard from any more museums needing you?"

"Nothing new. You know I just finished the contract for the museum in Cleveland. I need a break," she said.

Ricky's phone vibrated again.

"Same number as last time, Asheville," Ricky thought out loud.

"Well maybe you should put your rule to the side and go ahead and answer it. It might be a job," Susan said while giving him a look over the top of her reading glasses.

Ricky answered the phone, "Hello."

"This is Clif Jordan. I own the Circus Act Brewery in Asheville."

"Ok, what can I do for you?" Ricky snipped.

"Is this Ricky Temple the PI from over in High Point?" Clif asked.

"It's private investigator, and yes that's me. What can I do for you?"

"Some breweries up here are having some issues, and a mutual friend gave me your name as the guy to call."

"Who's the mutual friend?" Ricky asked. "I don't usually take cases that far west."

"I understand, I saw your territory map on your website. Father Tim Daniels said we needed to talk to Ricky Temple. Or as he calls you, Ricky T.," Clif added the Ricky T part to prove he had actually talked with Father Tim and hadn't just pulled his name off the internet.

"Tim Daniels?" Ricky said, which got Susan's attention too.

"Yeah, you do know him, don't you?" Clif asked.

"You could say we know each other," Ricky replied. "Look Clif, my wife and I are out of town and not at the house at moment. Could we set a call up for later today? Maybe 2:00? You can fill me in on your problem and we can go from there?"

"Sounds good, 2:00." Click.

Ricky first met Tim Daniels in kindergarten. They have been close friends ever since, more like brothers. Tim is a couple of years older than Ricky. After he graduated high school, he went off to Western Carolina University. A few years later, Ricky started there as well, and they ended up in the same fraternity. After graduation, Tim went on to graduate school and then law school. Eventually, Tim decided the law was not as much fun as it looked on TV and entered the seminary to become a Catholic priest. After his family, Ricky was the first person he called about his decision. As for Ricky, after graduation he tried working in the real world, as military people call it, for a short time but decided the military was the place for him. If Father Tim was putting this beer guy in touch with him, the least he could do is listen.

As they finished up their coffee and snack, Susan asked about the phone call.

"All I know right now is some breweries in Asheville are having issues with someone. Tim put these guys on to me. As you heard I set a phone call with him at 2:00 this afternoon," Ricky said.

"How about we head down to the outlet mall buy some stuff we probably don't need, then pick up some lunch? We can eat outside and enjoy the view of the Sound before we need to head home," Ricky said. He put his Sox hat back on indicating he was ready to leave.

"Sounds good."

They got into the BMW and Ricky selected the 80's satellite radio station. One of the songs that epitomized the 80's had just started, A-ha's 'Take on Me.' Ricky sang along, off-key as usual. He can't hit that famous high note, and truth be told he can't hit the low

11

notes either. Susan was dancing in her seat as they pulled onto Croatan Highway and headed south towards the outlet mall.

Fifteen minutes, 10 miles, and three and half butchered 80's songs later they pulled into the outlet mall and Ricky parked in front of the Polo Ralph Lauren store. He needed some new shirts but knew Susan would go straight to the Outer Banks Olive Oil shop and to stock up on their house made chocolates. If ever there was a woman with a sweet tooth it was Susan Temple. After they both did their shopping, they met up at the car.

"How about stopping at the Brewing Company and getting some burgers for lunch?" Ricky asked.

"That works, I'll call it in now so we can grab it and go," Susan offered. He wasn't as talkative so she could tell the phone call was on his mind. This probably meant there was a trip to Asheville coming her way.

After picking up lunch, Ricky went out the back of the parking lot to avoid the traffic on the main road. He turned onto Colington Road heading toward the Sound, mentally preparing for the phone call.

As they pulled into the driveway of their Outer Banks home, Ricky pushed the phone call button on the steering wheel. "Call Tim Daniels" was his command.

Tim's number rang several times and eventually went to voicemail. "Hey man, it's Ricky T. I got a call from a Clif Jordan who says he owns Circus Act Brewing up there in Asheville and you gave him my number. Give me a call." Click.

Like most Outer Banks homes, their two-story house on stilts had a screened-in porch on half of the space and the rest was uncovered for maximum sun burning. It had beautiful views of the Sound, which is why they had settled on this particular house. Ricky and Susan had just finished the burgers and were enjoying the calm of the sound and the quiet of October on the Outer Banks. "You're thinking about Asheville, aren't you?" she asked.

"I am. I guess we will both find out in a few minutes. When this guy calls, I'll put him on speakerphone so you can listen in. I know I don't have to tell you to take whatever notes you want. If you think I'm missing something, write it down and show me."

"So, the usual plan," she said.

"Nobody likes a smart ass," he quipped.

"Well, you're the one who married me," she shot back with a smirk.

Saved by the phone buzzing, Ricky looked at the number and then at Susan and gave her a nod indicating it was time for work.

"Ricky T. here."

"Ricky, its Clif Jordan calling back. Hope you have some time."

"Sure do, I'm going to put you on speakerphone so my wife can listen in, if that works."

"No problem. A few of the breweries up here are having some problems with a group of locals. At least we think that's who is behind it. It started with a boycott, but last night someone broke in and opened the taps which drained a lot of beer. As of now, they are going after us economically. Hopefully it doesn't go further." Clif continued, "We aren't sure who is behind it, which is why we are calling you."

"To be honest," Ricky said, "this sounds more like a problem for the Asheville Police Department or the Buncombe County Sherriff. Also, do you mind filling me in on how you know Father Tim?"

"Sure, Father Tim comes by some of the downtown businesses from time to time. Circus Act Brewery is one of his usual stops, he likes our stout. He comes in after mass on Sundays to catch his Carolina Panthers. He tries to keep up with what's going on downtown and the business owners like that about him. I've known him for years and he was one of the first people I met when I opened my brewery. As for the Police Department, we called them and agree that it falls on them. They are working on this, but their manpower is low at the moment. Two other owners and I met and decided we want someone who works for us to investigate and let us know what's going on. More importantly, we want it stopped before it goes any further."

Ricky looked at Susan who shrugged her shoulders and gave him a slight head tilt as if to say she wasn't sure about all this.

"Clif," Ricky said, "I'm not sure it's a good idea for a private investigator to get involved in what should be a police matter, even one as good as me." Susan rolled her eyes as Ricky gave her a smirk that said he was just screwing around with this guy.

"Ricky, I hear you but all we are asking is that you come up to Asheville, meet with us and hear what we have to say before you decide. If it helps, there is already a room reserved for you, on us, at The Grove Park Inn for four nights. And there is check for five hundred dollars for you to just listen."

Susan mouthed, "The Grove Park Inn."

Ricky mouthed back, "Five hundred dollars."

Anybody who knows about Asheville knows about The Grove Park Inn. Listed as a national historic site, it was built by Edwin Grove on land he bought in 1900. Sitting on Sunset Mountain, the Inn opened in 1913. It was made of granite off the mountain that was moved up to the site one piece at a time, mainly by horse-pulled wagons. The Inn has a grand hall made of stone with fireplaces the size of trees. Ricky and his family had sat in front of those fireplaces on several Christmas Eves, and it brought back fond memories thinking of those rocking chairs. The Inn has beautiful views of the sunset and great restaurants. Since it's opening it has had many famous guests such as F. Scott Fitzgerald, John Ford, and several recent and past Presidents.

"Well Clif, that's very generous. When is the reservation?"

"Friday through Monday, how does that sound?" Clif responded.

"That doesn't work for us. We are in Kill Devil Hills until Saturday. If you can change the reservation, send the confirmation to my email. If I get that, I'll call you and give you an answer."

"Let me see what I can do. It should be easy since my wife is the reservation manager." Click.

Turning to Susan, Ricky asked, "What do you think?"

"Hard to say. It doesn't seem like much but if we get four free days at the Grove Park Inn and five hundred dollars, hell, why not. We just got confirmation for the change to our reservation. It's under your name and is for Sunday through Wednesday, checking out on Thursday. What do you think now?" she asked.

"I think we are going to Asheville."

Early Saturday morning, Ricky and Susan finished packing the car to start the seven-hour drive from Kill Devil Hills to Asheville. They decided the night before they would make a quick stop at their condo in High Point. They needed to swap their beach clothes for mountain clothes, and to get everything they needed for business trips like Susan's computers and Ricky's gear.

They pulled up to the stop light at Colington Road to turn right on to South Croatan Highway. Ten miles later they made the big sweeping right onto Highway 64 and crossed the first bridge at Wanchese and Manteo, then went across the second bridge through the Alligator River National Wildlife Refuge. A third bridge brought them to the mainland of North Carolina, and they were on their way. Ricky hoped to pull into the condo in five hours and 30 minutes.

Ricky turned down the 80's channel and started thinking out loud to Susan. "We have time, so we should get some research done and get as smart as we can. See what you can find about this Clif

Jordan, when the brewery boom started in Asheville, and when the tourist boom started as well."

Susan whipped out her phone while saying, "I'll also look at the news to see what's going on up there, if anything." Within a few minutes Susan had some initial results. Ricky was always impressed by how great a researcher his wife is.

"Not much coming up on the Circus Act Brewing website about Clif Jordan, but here are the highlights. He moved to Asheville around 2009 from Maryland. In 2010 he got financing and opened Circus Act Brewing. It's located on the South Slope. It struggled a bit at first but has become a very popular brewery stop for tourists."

"First of all, what the hell is the South Slope? I grew up in Asheville and I've never heard of the South Slope."

"I was wondering the same thing. Google maps show it as an area downtown. Basically, a triangle from the middle of town, around Patton Avenue if that means anything to you, going south down a hill towards a baseball stadium for several blocks."

"So that slight downhill from downtown towards the baseball stadium and the hospitals is now a slope? Ok."

The car fell silent again. Ricky noticed Susan was making notes but wasn't saying anything. This could mean she was finding what they were looking for, or she was hungry.

"I'm hungry, can we stop and get something to eat?" she said.

"What about that chocolate you bought yesterday?"

"I ate it already," she admitted.

"There are only fast-food spots around here. We won't be near any restaurants until we get closer to Raleigh."

"Fast food is fine, as long as I can get a salad."

After stopping for a quick lunch, they continued toward the condo. As they got closer to Raleigh, the clouds began to darken. Ricky thought that was fitting since he didn't think much of the capital city. As they got to the east side of town, the sprinkles became a steady rain and eventually a downpour. As usual, the traffic moving around Raleigh was heavy and dumb. People were cutting others off, going 80 or 90 mph, driving inches from bumpers all in a heavy downpour. Ricky was not enjoying this drive, but they only had about an hour and half to the condo.

When they finally cleared Raleigh and left the heaviest rain behind them, Susan saw some of Ricky's anxiety melt away. She said she had more background information for him.

"From what I can tell, the first brewery opened around 1994 and started in the basement of a restaurant on Biltmore Avenue on the South Slope, now that we know what that is. During the next several years, downtown came alive with a few more restaurants and bars opening. The real boom seems to have hit in the early 2000s when several more breweries popped up and tourists started finding out about Asheville for more than just the Biltmore House. As of now, there are over 50 breweries in and around Asheville, hence the nickname Beer City. Over the years there was a slow increase in real estate prices as it became a playground for rich tourists. Recently, the Asheville Regional Airport expanded with direct flights from New York, Boston, Chicago, and major cities in Florida. Now there is a constant flow of out-of-staters," she paused.

"Fifty breweries, you have got to be kidding me. How is that sustainable?" Ricky asked. "So, if I'm hearing you right, tourists are coming in big numbers, deciding to stay, buying up the real estate, and drinking beer."

"Yes," she said. "And let's remember that during Covid, North Carolina was a prime spot for people moving out of New York, New Jersey, Maryland, and Pennsylvania, among many others. Things are cheaper down here. People can sell their house up north, come down here, and get a similar house that should cost

$250K but spend $800K thus destroying the market. It's crazy. One last thing, there is also a City Council election going on."

Ricky fell quiet and absorbed the information, mainly because they were only about 20 minutes from their driveway. He wanted to pack quickly and get back on the road. It was time to see Asheville in person, for the first time in a long time.

Ricky and Susan worked efficiently. They had done this before. While Susan packed clothes for the mountain weather, Ricky put the BMW in the garage and covered it. Then he pulled out the silver Ford Escape. When he started his investigation business, Ricky did some research and determined the Ford Escape to be the perfect work car. There were lots of them on the road so he could blend in when needed. He made sure the gas tank was full, then went inside to help Susan. When they were finished, they had managed to be at the condo for only two hours.

"When we get going again, will you look up hotel rooms up there? If we decide to stay, we will need a place after our four days of luxury are over," Ricky said.

Susan left Ricky alone to drive and continue to process the information she had found, as well as hum to the 80s station, off-key.

"Damn!" Susan yelled. "Hotel rooms in Asheville are between $400 and $600 a night. No wonder people aren't happy with this place," she said. "I can't find anything reasonably priced. We would have to stay outside of town and I'm sure that's not what you want."

"Let's try VRBO or that other site, you know the one I always forget," Ricky suggested.

"Ok, I think I have something. I found a house in North Asheville we can rent for three weeks. Compared to the hotels, it's affordable."

"Grab it while it's still available and try for a month. We have no idea how long this will take but verify the cancellation policy," he said.

Interstate-40 is such a boring drive, Ricky thought. Just a long
straight road with nothing to look at. After a couple of hours and a
few stops, they were at the base of Old Fort Mountain. He felt
better when he saw the exit for Old Fort because once up the
mountain, he would be almost done with driving for the day. It's a
six-mile climb from bottom to top, then another thirty minutes to
The Grove Park Inn. Forty-five minutes later, Ricky was happy
again when the I-240 Exit off I-40 came up. It had been a long day.
His relaxation didn't last long because out of nowhere a Mercedes
SUV cut in front of them with a few feet to spare.

"What the hell was that?" Ricky yelled. Then a few minutes later, it
happened again. This time it was a Subaru. "Did you notice both of
those cars had out of state license plates?" Ricky asked. "Now
what? Why is the traffic stopping? We have only been off the
interstate about a half a mile. There must be an accident up there."
After thirty minutes of stop and go traffic and no accident in sight,
they made it to exit 5B. He got off the exit and turned right to
Charlotte Street, feeling relieved again to be off the highway, but it
was short lived.

"Man, there are people everywhere. Driving, biking, jay walking,
this place has changed a lot. Look at this." They continued down
Charlotte Street and passed the Manor, where Ricky's family used
to go swimming during the summer. He told Susan, for the tenth
time, that it not only was a swimming club, but it was also used as
the British Headquarters for the movie 'The Last of the Mohicans.'
At St. Mary's Episcopal Church, they turned right on to Macon
Avenue and drove up the mountain a few miles until it crested at
the entrance to The Grove Park Inn. They stopped and told the
security guard they were checking in and he waved them through.
A very tired and road weary Ricky and Susan went down the
narrow roadway winding towards the entrance. They were in Beer
City.

Chapter 3

"Good afternoon, Asheville, I'm Darby Jones. Thanks for choosing to get your news from WAVL. Asheville Police are investigating Thursday's breaking and entering and vandalism at a few downtown breweries. Investigators tell us they still do not have any leads and ask if anyone knows anything about this to contact the Asheville Police Department. There's an accident on Merrimon Avenue near the post office and McDonald's causing delays. If you are going downtown, you might want to use an alternate route. The wreckage is expected to be cleared within the next hour. The other big story we are following for you is the Asheville City Council elections. As you know, incumbents Bobbi Carnes and Phil Bradley are up for reelection. We also know Nick Zika, owner of the wildly popular South Asheville restaurant, Pappas Greek Table, is a candidate. Election day is still several weeks away and so far, it's been a quiet campaign season. Join us tonight at six for more on these stories and a cute video a viewer sent in of a family of deer. Enjoy the rest of your Sunday afternoon."

Bobbi Carnes took a sip of her herbal tea and turned off her TV as the update ended, going back to trying to relax on her only day off. She grabbed her phone and called her fellow council member Phil Bradley. "Hey, how's it going? Did you see the news about the vandalism downtown?" she asked.

"Yeah, I don't think it's anything to worry about. I'm sure the police have it under control," Phil said. "Our reelection is shaping up to be not much more than a formality. With all the experience we bring from down south and out west, I think we are safe. So far, the only new candidate I know of is Nick Zika. I mean let's face it, he has the hottest restaurant in town, but I don't know that he knows anything about local government. There is another candidate, I can't remember who it is though, he hasn't organized a campaign yet."

"We need to keep an eye on these attacks downtown. We don't need a mess during election season. Let's meet up this week for lunch," Bobbi said as she took a sip of her herbal tea. "Does Wednesday work for you?"

"Wednesday is good at the usual spot," Phil said, and hung up.

Ronnie Jenkins pulled his dark grey Toyota 4Runner into Billy's driveway on Mills Place in Woodfin. He parked in his usual spot next to Billy's Bronco and walked around the back of the house to the basement door. Over the years, Billy had turned the basement into a bar for the Boys. They used it mainly to watch sports and to discuss important things in private. Ronnie saw Jimmy's white Ford truck, so he knew he was already there. They were waiting for Dave.

Ronnie walked under the Western Carolina University flag that hung over the door, tapped it with his hand like they all did when they walked in, and took his usual seat. They each had selected their spot when Billy was designing the bar. Ronnie and Jimmy had recliners on the left side with clear views of the TV and the bar. Billy built the bar on the right side of the room just a few feet from the door Ronnie had just walked in. Dave liked sitting at the bar and had a very comfortable bar chair that he could swivel to talk to whoever was playing bartender or towards the room and the TV. Billy put bronze placards on the back of the chairs with their names.

Billy Thompson had lived in the house for most of his life, except for when he was away with the Boys at college. When his mother passed away, he inherited the house and started the slow but difficult process of making it his own. At the time he was still new to the pool business, so he didn't have a lot of money for renovations. Instead, he spent his time planning. It was one of his lasting memories of his mother which made it difficult to change, but over time he saved money and made peace with his decisions.

Recently, he was promoted to crew chief and the remodel moved quicker. A neon Busch Light sign was the latest addition. Now there was talk among the crew that Billy would be made Vice President of the company. His hard work was paying off. Life was going well for Billy and the only real annoyance was the occasional realtor dropping by and asking if he wanted to sell, at a huge profit of course. Usually, those conversations ended with the door being shut in the realtor's face.

"Did you watch the games yesterday?" Billy asked Ronnie.

"There were some great games, so I stayed up way too late. Where the hell is Dave? Don't we have some things to talk about?" Ronnie asked. He was mad because even on a Sunday, it took him twice as long to get to Billy's because of all the leaf peepers. He was also still a little hung over from the night before.

"All that rain last week put us behind, so Dave is out finishing some lawns we couldn't get to. He'll be here in about an hour or so," Jimmy answered.

Jimmy and Dave's lawn business had taken off. They now had enough business to hire more people. On an average day they had three full crews out working properties. Jimmy and Dave were hands-on owners and they each led a crew. Trent Burns, who was one of Dave's first hires, leads the third crew. When they could, Dave and Jimmy slipped away and did estimates for new business.

Ronnie sat in his chair and thought about how far they had all come. Billy really has done well with the pool company and Jimmy and Dave's landscaping business was booming. As for Ronnie, starting out as a loan officer was tough at first. He gritted his teeth and after working on personal loans for a few years, he was moved to mortgages which changed everything. Ronnie enjoyed mortgages much more and eventually he was made the lead of the mortgage team. A few years into working mortgages, he noticed a lot of the locals were applying for mortgages but were being turned down. They had good credit but with the real estate prices going higher each year and interest rates fluctuating, locals were not qualifying.

Then he noticed a disturbing trend, most applications had out-of-town addresses. He did not like this new development.

Eventually, Ronnie became the branch manager. He quickly found that even as the branch manager, there was little he could do to help the locals. He came up with a new idea to help his hometown.

"Dave knows where our project stands but we'll still wait for him to make any decisions. I think the boycott of the breweries is having some effect, but not enough. Breweries, hippies, and tourists invade downtown from late spring through early fall. We lose our city for six months a year. It added 15 minutes to my drive to work. They stand in the road, cross the street without looking. People who have been here for generations, like our families and our friends' families, can barely afford to live here anymore. It's out of control. We went from being Cool Green Asheville to chaos. I think it's time to look at new ideas. We need to get our nice quiet mountain town back," Ronnie preached.

"I'm ready to up the game," Jimmy said. Although Jimmy O'Brien was considered Ronnies right hand man, he was also one of the more levelheaded of the group except when it came to his hometown. "I agree with getting Asheville back. Hell, we all want the small town back, but let's talk this through."

After landing at the Asheville Regional Airport, Brenda and Eddie Carletti walked into the Coxe Ave Brewery and found a place to sit near a TV showing the NFL games. "It's a cool looking place," Eddie thought, with a long oak bar, some tables, and big windows looking into the brewing area.

Brenda liked the open garage door allowing the cool late September air in. 'Good thing I brought a sweater,' she thought. They stood out a bit, wearing New York Giants football jerseys, but they didn't care because today was a big game. Their Giants were playing the Cowboys. Eddie ordered the IPA and Brenda asked for the lightest beer they had and a glass of water. The bar was about half full, which was fine with them. It would be easier to watch the game and get refills.

Brenda and Eddie live in Oyster Bay on Long Island. The direct flight from JFK landed at 11:00 a.m., but by the time they got their bags and rental car and drove the 40 minutes into the city, it was after 1:00. Lucky for Brenda and Eddie the hotel was not far from the tap room they had read about in the travel magazine. As they got their beers, the game was in the beginning of the second quarter and the Cowboys were up by seven points.

Brenda could tell the two couples at the other end of the bar were from up north as well. She guessed Long Island, like them. She was right and eventually the two groups merged, even though they were Jets fans.

"Well, what do you think of Asheville so far?" Eddie asked Brenda.

"It's cute! I loved the views we had driving in and getting the mountain view room was worth the extra money. It was easy getting down here and the flight went by fast. People seem to be nice, but they keep talking about how cool it is. They need to come up to New York and experience real fall weather. What about you?" Brenda asked.

"I like it a lot. From what I saw online, I don't think we could afford this kind of life permanently, but it's good for a weekend getaway. Geez, I can't believe the Giants are losing," Eddie said, changing the subject. "Hey, bartender another IPA," he demanded.

"Take it easy sport, these beers have a high alcohol content," the bartender said.

"Don't worry about it, I know what I'm doing," he responded arrogantly, while rolling his eyes at Brenda. "Can you believe this guy?"

At halftime, the Giants were down 14 points. Eddie was pissed, partially because the beers were taking effect, giving him a shorter fuse, and partially because his Giants were losing. They ordered another beer hoping the second half would be better.

"What are we doing tomorrow?" Eddie asked.

"Depends on what time we wake up. That article I read said there are some good coffee shops near the hotel. After that, I thought we could go look at some of the local art. It sounds like there's great art and pottery in the area. I wouldn't mind looking around and seeing what downtown has to offer. Then in the afternoon, I set up one of those walking beer tours. I thought you would like that," Brenda said hoping for a quick agreement from Eddie.

"Art, really? Ok, let's do it. Sounds like a plan."

The rain had made his long week that much longer, Dave was thinking as he finished a lawn in South Asheville. He and Jimmy had agreed they would avoid working weekends as much as they could but knew it would happen. As he put his equipment on the truck, he felt better knowing he only had one more lawn today. After that, he could meet up with the Boys and maybe catch some of the late NFL games if Jimmy wasn't watching his crush, Darby Jones, on the news. He wouldn't mind a cold beer, too.

While Dave drove to the last stop of the day, he texted Jimmy to let him know where he was. He didn't have a crew with him, so each job was taking longer. Jimmy had offered to go with him, but Dave wanted at least one of them to have a day off.

Dave went over the other business in his head. The combination of the boycott and dumping beer seemed to be working, but it wasn't enough. Dumping the beer got some attention but he thought it was odd the boycott wasn't in the news. Like the others, he was tired of the new Asheville and each year it seemed to be getting worse. After work one evening, he and Jimmy had scouted out a warehouse down near the French Broad River that a few of the breweries used to store their supplies. Not a lot of people knew about the warehouse and the breweries hoped it stayed that way. They didn't want people breaking in and stealing their supplies. As a business owner, Dave thought their approach made sense. Destroying the supplies, or the entire warehouse, would hurt production and would send a message. It would be an easy hit if they wanted.

As he often did, Dave thought about his parents. When the city and county taxes kept going up, they had to sell their house and move into the country. They had almost been foreclosed on and were forced to sell with the profits going to back taxes. Dave never forgot this. He and Sara Dunn, his fiancée, moved Dave's parents in to help them out. They lived with Dave and Sara until they passed away a few years ago. He always loved Sara for putting his parents first.

Dave and Sara first met at the festival that takes over downtown the last weekend in July. Sara had been there with a group of friends and Dave was there with the Boys. She wasn't model skinny, but she was not large either, more like the girl next door, which Dave liked. They were standing on opposite sides of the stage listening to a classic rock band play. Sara noticed Dave long before he noticed her. By the time the band played its encore, which was an attempt at Led Zeppelin's D'yer Mak'er, they were focused on each other. That was 10 years ago, and they are still together. Dave loved Sara but wasn't sure they would ever get married. They were happy with the way things were. They always said if they got married their first dance would be D'yer Mak'er.

By the end of the third quarter the Giants were down 21 and there was no sign the offense was going to make an appearance today. They decided they were done. Eddie found himself spending more time thinking about the beer and less time thinking about the game. He was comfortable in this bar. Like most places, the music at Coxe Ave Brewery depended on who was behind the bar. They picked a good night, and the bartender was playing a lot of reggae. It also didn't hurt to have met some people from home. It was shaping up to be a good weekend for Brenda and Eddie.

"How about we get one more beer and then find a place for dinner?" Brenda suggested. "I want to try some real North Carolina barbecue. I heard there is a good spot not too far from here."

"Let's just go, this game is over. We can get some food and start over tomorrow."

They paid for their beers and said goodbye to their new friends after making plans to meet up for Monday Night Football. Brenda went to the bathroom while Eddie started towards the door. They met up outside and walked across the street to where they parked the blue Camry they rented.

Eddie started the car to get the heat going while Brenda looked up the address for the barbecue restaurant. "It's just a couple of minutes' drive. We could probably walk if we wanted," Brenda said.

Eddie thought it would be quicker to drive. It was getting cooler, and he wanted the car close by after they ate. Eddie pulled out of the parking space and worked his way to the front of the parking lot. He had to wait a few minutes for the traffic to clear and then turned left. As they approached the stop light it turned red. Brenda noticed Eddie was straddling the double yellow line but decided not to say anything. She knew Eddie usually drank Coors Light, so maybe the craft beers were affecting him more than she thought. The light turned green. Eddie started going but was startled when he heard a horn honking at him from a car coming in the other direction. "What's wrong with that asshole?" he yelled as he jerked the car back into his lane.

Dave was on the phone with Jimmy letting him know he'd finished the last job of the day and was on his way. He was excited because the customer at the last stop gave them a nice end-of-season tip. Dave knew Sara would be very happy about the extra money, so he decided to text her about it the next time he stopped. Jimmy gave him a heads up that Ronnie and Billy wanted to talk about escalation when he got there.

"Ok, sounds good to me. I'm in. Hey, I'm heading up Biltmore Avenue and just passed the hospital, I'll see you guys in about 15 or 20 minutes depending on traffic."

Dave was rolling along now and knew all he needed was to turn on South Charlotte Street and traffic would calm down. He had a green light, so he put on his turn signal and started his turn. Suddenly, he saw a flash of blue from his left.

Eddie and Brenda were coming up to the Biltmore Avenue intersection and Brenda was not happy since he missed the turn again. For the third time, she thought walking would've been quicker. She knew he had a few beers in him, but she didn't know how unclearly he was thinking. As they got to the intersection, Brenda looked up from her phone and saw the light was red.

"NOOOO STOP!" she yelled. It was too late. A white pickup truck was making a right turn and Eddie ran the light. He didn't have the time to hit the brakes and was heading right for the driver's door of the truck.

Jimmy and Billy were getting restless. They wanted a beer, but they all had agreed that there was no drinking when they were going to discuss business. Having a clear head when making decisions was important. Billy didn't like the rule, but Ronnie had insisted. This way nobody could say they didn't remember what they had agreed to.

"It's been an hour. Was Dave stopping for food or something?" Ronnie asked.

"Not that I know of. If he isn't here in a few minutes, I'll give him a call. Maybe he stopped to see Sara and drop off that tip money," Jimmy said.

"Screw it, I'm calling, we've got things to talk about," Jimmy said as he picked up his phone.

Jimmy hit his speed dial for Dave and the other end started ringing. After a few rings the other end picked up and then, "Hello."

"Hey, where the hell are you?" Jimmy asked.

"Who is this?" was the response.

It took Jimmy a few seconds to realize it wasn't Dave's voice.

"This is Jimmy, put Dave on the phone." Something wasn't right. Jimmy started shaking as panic set in. Why was someone else answering Dave's phone? The look on Jimmy's face and his voice told the others that something wasn't right. They edged over to try to hear what was going on.

"This is Officer Clark of the Asheville Police Department. Are you a friend of Dave Finley's?"

"We are business partners and we've been friends for as long as I can remember. Why is the APD answering Dave's phone?" Jimmy asked. Jimmy could hear people shouting orders and sirens in the background. It sounded like chaos.

"Mr. O'Brien, I'm sorry to have to inform you but your friend was involved in a serious automobile accident. He didn't make it."

Jimmy dropped the phone. Then his head. All he could do was to keep repeating, "No way, no way, no way."

"What? What?! WHERE'S DAVE? I want to talk to Dave right now," Billy yelled.

Ronnie, trying to keep calm, picked up the phone.

"This is Ronnie Jenkins, who is this?"

"Like I was telling that last person, I'm Officer Clark with the Asheville Police Department. Are you another friend of Mr. Finley's?"

"Yes. What happened?"

"It's early but it appears a blue Camry ran a red light at a high rate of speed and hit Mr. Finley directly in the driver's side door. Mr. Finley was pronounced dead at the scene. Who is his next of kin?"

Now Ronnie was shaking but he was able to keep it together. "He is engaged to Sara Dunn. They live in Weaverville. Then there's us. Billy Thompson, Jimmy O'Brien, and myself. We're coming down there. Where did this guy kill Dave? What happened to the other driver?" Jimmy asked.

"I wouldn't come down here, it is not a pretty sight. As for the other driver and passenger, it was a male and female, they are in critical condition at the hospital. The car is a rental. There is a strong smell of alcohol in the car. Stay there, Mr. Jenkins, there is nothing you can do here. Mr. Finley's body will be taken to the morgue and then to the Asheville Funeral Home over on Merrimon Avenue when it's released. The best thing you can do is support his fiancée and help her make arrangements for his service. What's your phone number in case we need to talk to someone?"

Ronnie gave the officer his number and hung up. "I wonder why Bobby was being so formal on the phone?" he thought out loud.

"Dave's dead. Some fucking drunk tourist killed Dave," is all Ronnie could manage to say. Nobody knew what to say or do. They were all in shock. Several minutes had passed when Billy said they needed to get over to Sara. She needed to hear this from them and not the police. They all agreed and got in Jimmy's truck to drive the few minutes over to Dave and Sara's house in Weaverville.

Sara knew something was wrong as soon as she saw the three of them get out of the truck. They all had the same look on their faces. She had been trying to call and text Dave, but the phone had been busy and then it went straight to voicemail. Ronnie walked up to Sara as Jimmy and Billy stood beside her and told her the news. Sara let out a loud long scream as she fell to the ground. The guys let her sit on the ground for a few minutes before they helped her up and into the house.

That night, nobody slept. As one person pulled themselves together, someone else broke down. Nobody went to work on Monday. There were too many things to do. They all needed to be with each other, especially Sara.

Early the next morning, they sat in silence and had coffee while trying to regroup. Sara had finally dozed off again at about 8:30. Word of the accident was getting out and now it was all over the news. Friends and neighbors were starting to drop by the house. In true southern tradition, everyone brought food and offered Sara any help she needed. It was getting to be too much, so Billy ran interference at the front door. They tried to get Sara to go back to sleep, but she could only manage an hour.
A combination of the phone, doorbell, and grief kept her from much more than that.

Ten o'clock brought another knock on the door and Billy went to get rid of whoever it was. A few seconds later, Billy appeared in the living room with Officer Miller from the police department.

"Sorry to bother you under the circumstances. Ms. Dunn, I'm very sorry for your loss. I know this is a hard time, but I have a few questions to complete my report," Officer Miller said. "Can you tell me where Mr. Finley was yesterday?"

Jimmy didn't want Sara to have to talk to the police, so he answered. "He was working down in South Asheville. Dave and I own Cats Landscaping. The rain last week put us behind, so he was catching up on the jobs we missed. I talked to him around 4:00 when he was finishing up and getting ready to drive to Billy's house over in Woodfin to meet us. We told the officer all this last night. Why do we have to go over it all again?"

"Instead of questioning us, you need to be interrogating the people who killed Dave. Have they been arrested yet?" Billy yelled, standing up and pointing at the officer. Ronnie walked over and put a hand on Billy's shoulder, letting him know that now was not the time.

"What can you tell us?" asked Sara.

"The driver of the other car is still unconscious but expected to be ok. The passenger is awake and talking. They are from Oyster Bay on Long Island, and they flew in early yesterday for a weekend getaway. They had been to Coxe Ave Brewery to watch football and were on their way to get some barbecue for dinner when the accident happened. The driver had twice the allowed alcohol amount in his blood. The two of them were supposed to fly back to New York tomorrow. That won't be happening," Officer Miller told them. "Mr. Finley's body will be released to the funeral home tomorrow morning. Is the one on Merrimon Avenue ok with you?" he asked.

"I guess, it's not something we ever talked about," Sara responded. She broke down again and then left the room.

After offering his condolences again, Officer Miller left.

When he was gone, Ronnie, Billy and Jimmy huddled outside by Jimmy's truck. Looking around to ensure nobody was within earshot, Jimmy said, "Some fucking drunk from New York ran a light and killed Dave. I'm done with these tourists taking over our town. They'll probably get some high-priced New York lawyer and get off free. It's time to act."

They got in Jimmy's truck and drove back to Billy's. Ronnie didn't say much more after his outburst at Sara's. It was obvious he was thinking things over. Once there, the three of them stood beside Ronnie's 4Runner. "It's time to escalate," Ronnie said. "No texts, no phone calls, we only discuss it face to face. Billy, you head downtown later and keep an eye on that tap room, see what you can find out. I will check on Sara in a few hours and help her with planning a service for Dave. The circle is closed, what we say stays between the three of us."

"I'll go with Billy," Jimmy said as he got back into his truck. Jimmy drove off for his house to get a shower, a change of clothes and some sleep before he and Billy started their surveillance.

Ronnie jumped in his 4Runner and left for his house a few miles away. He was barely keeping it together.

Billy turned and walked into his house. He hated what their city had become. He also knew this wasn't the time to turn the heat up, but Dave had been killed. He decided enough was enough.

Chapter 4

When Ricky and Susan got off the elevator, they had a decision to make. If they turned right, they would be at the breakfast buffet. If they turned left, they would be in the main lobby also known as the Grand Hall. The Grand Hall features two large fireplaces at each end, a line of rocking chairs in front of them, and multiple sofas and chairs throughout. It was a great place to sit for morning coffee.

After a brief discussion, they turned left and headed for the Grand Hall then decided to sit outside on The Sunset Terrace. It was cool for late September, but it felt great, and the view was incredible. Ricky got some coffee while Susan picked two seats. There was fog hanging on the mountains off in the distance, but the peaks still rose above making for a spectacular morning view. If you looked slightly to the left, you could see downtown Asheville as it was slowly coming alive for another day. The view in front them was down the fairway of one of the golf course holes. Just beyond the flagstick was a street with what appeared to be very nice houses. They were beginning to understand why people came here.

There was no conversation for a while, they just soaked it all in. After a coffee refill Susan broke the silence. "What time is your meeting downtown?"

"One. But I'm going to get an early lunch here and then drive around a bit to get a feel. Care to join me for lunch?" he asked.

"Can't, I have a spa appointment at eleven and I can get food there." They finished their second cup of coffee and reluctantly decided to go back to the room.

As they walked back into the lobby, Ricky asked the concierge to bring his car up at noon. With that done he turned to Susan and said, "Tomorrow morning, I vote we sit in front of the fireplace."

"Sounds good to me."

Inside their room, Ricky went to the refrigerator to get a bottle of water, and Susan turned on the local news to see if anything was going on.

"Ricky, you need to see this," she said.

"Asheville Police confirm speed and alcohol were a factor in the accident that killed local businessman, Dave Finley. The investigation is ongoing but formal charges are expected to be filed in the next couple of days. Tensions are high in the city after last night's accident and last week's vandalism at two breweries. Asheville Police urge residents to not take the law into their own hands and to let them continue their investigation. This has been a WAVL news break. We hope to see you at noon. I'm Darby Jones, WAVL news."

"That's not going to help things. There's already tension and now a local was killed by a tourist. Things could get interesting quickly," Ricky said. "After your spa and fancy lunch, would you dig into this accident and the driver, Dave Finley, I think she said?" Ricky asked.

"Got it."

Ricky put on his good jeans, his String Cheese Incident t-shirt, and his trusty Birkenstocks. He grabbed his Red Sox hat as he headed to the lobby for a quick lunch. Sitting in Edison Grill he mulled everything over. He ate his burger quickly because he decided he needed to see downtown before the meeting. Ricky signed the lunch bill to his room and walked through the lobby to his waiting car. He tipped the valet and drove to the exit taking him back down Macon Avenue to Charlotte Street. Since he was already on Charlotte Street, he decided to stay on it and drive past the scene of the accident. This would put him close to the Coxe Ave Brewery where his meeting was.

"I don't know where he is," Clif said. "He'll be here."

"While we wait, fill us in on this guy again," Mike said.

"Father Tim said they've known each other since elementary school. Ricky is from here but hasn't spent much time in town since he graduated from Western Carolina and went into the military. Ricky was what they call a comm guy in the Army. He worked on radios, networks, computers, satellite communications stuff like that. After a few years he joined some special secret thing. Father Tim referred to it as The Command. Ricky became a special operations communicator and did all the overseas stuff, Iraq, and Afghanistan. At some point, he was working with an intelligence team and there was a major attack against a U.S. base, so he jumped in. He showed a knack for intelligence, so he transferred and did comms for an intelligence group at The Command. Not sure what all that means, But I trust Father Tim. The last thing Father Tim said was to not underestimate Ricky Temple."

As if on cue, Ricky walked in. "Sorry I'm late. I got stuck in traffic on the North Slope trying to get to the South Slope. Crazy." Ricky looked around the tap room. His first thought was, for 1:00 on a Monday during leaf season, the place was empty. His second thought was the few people here looked like they had fallen out of an LL Bean catalog. He hadn't seen that much flannel and rubber rain boots in his life, especially since it wasn't raining.

"There is no North Slope," Mike said.

Clif introduced everyone. When he was done, he asked Ricky if he wanted a drink.

"A bourbon neat would be great."

"It's a beer hall, so no bourbon," Mike said.

"Oh, that makes sense," Ricky said. "How about Miller High Life? It's the champagne of beer you know."

"Maybe a glass of water would be best," Clif decided.

"Sounds great. Ok, tell me what's going on that you wanted me up here." Ricky said.

Mike Lamb is a short stocky guy, and Ricky was thinking that he enjoyed his own beer. Mike took the lead. "It started about nine months ago. We got word a group of locals were talking about boycotting the downtown breweries. Seems they aren't happy with all the tourists and the growth around town. My brewery, Asheville Beer Facility, is still new but not the newest brewery between us, so I don't have much room for a boycott. I tried to figure out who was behind it but never got anywhere. Then, last week someone broke into mine and Clif's places and opened our taps, draining beer. We not only lost the beer but had to close for the day too. After the death of the landscape guy, we are starting to hear rumblings about escalation, but nothing's happened yet. I think something is coming. I was against hiring you, to be honest, but with this latest problem I'm glad we did."

"Are you from Asheville, Mike?" Ricky asked.

"No, Colorado."

Ricky glanced over at Brian Johnson. He was stocky too but taller than the others. Probably around six two and was the quiet one of the group. He hadn't said anything since the introductions. Ricky picked up a vibe from him that he couldn't place so he just registered it in the back of his mind.

"What about you, Brian? Where are you from?" Ricky asked.

Upstate New York was his response. He said he moved down 20 years ago and decided to make a go of it with Coxe Ave Brewery. It had been going well up until nine months ago.

"So, Clif is from Maryland, Brian is a New Yorker, a Yankees fan I assume," Ricky said, adjusting his Red Sox hat, "and Mike is from Colorado. Any reason the three of you are the ones being targeted?"

Brian said, "We have been vocal about our support of the City Council's plans for the future of the town. We think they have the town headed in the right direction. I think the town should be putting as much money as possible into tourism, but I know that doesn't sit well with some of the locals. It's not the quiet mountain town they all had grown up with, but progress is progress and I'm all for it. And as you just pointed out, none of us are originally from here, so maybe they are holding that against us, too."

"I can see that. You three have to understand that if I take this case, I do things my way. I know you are paying me, but I operate my way, and I don't take suggestions. All three of you need to agree to that. Thanks for putting us up at the Inn by the way, that was a nice touch. Lastly, if I were you, I would consider investing in Miller High Life and Chablis for my wife while we are in town," Ricky said with a grin.

"Don't get too excited about The Grove Park Inn. Since my wife works there, she gets large discounts on nightly rates. I suppose we could all agree the Miller High Life is your bonus," Clif said, smiling back at Ricky.

Ricky said he would poke around for a few days and told them if the case developed into anything he would work at a reduced fee as a favor to Father Tim. The three business owners appreciated his gesture, and they agreed on his reduced fee which included discounted Miller High Life for him and Chablis for Susan. They exchanged contact information, and he told them he would be in touch.

Ricky walked out of the Coxe Ave Brewery and crossed the street to the parking lot, not realizing he was following the same path as Brenda and Eddie a couple of nights earlier. As he got to his car, he felt a presence behind him, but it was too late to react.

"Who are you and why were you meeting with those three guys?" a voice said.

"I'm Peter Pan. Who the fuck are you?" Ricky snapped back. Ricky was mad. More at himself for not picking up on the guy behind him than anything else.

"I'm asking the questions. Now who are you and why were you meeting those three guys? I'm not asking again. I'm already in a bad mood," the voice responded. Not getting an answer fast enough, the guy decided to send a message by punching Ricky's kidneys.

"I already told you," Ricky started but didn't get to finish. The guy behind him hit him over the head a couple of times with some sort of blunt object.

"Some advice for you, tourist. We don't want you here. Go see orange and red leaves somewhere else. All grocery stores sell beer so there is no need to come here for the breweries. If you are working for those guys, I will find out. I won't be happy about it either. Take my advice and go home, tourist," the voice said.

With another whack on the head, Ricky went down. When he hit the ground, the second guy kicked him in the ribs and his back a few times. They finished him off with another crack on the head for good measure. Ricky was out cold.

Not sure how long he had been laying there, Ricky felt a slight nudge. It wasn't violent so he assumed it was someone else.

"Are you ok sir?" asked Officer Clark.

"Who are you?" asked Ricky.

"I'm Officer Clark of the Asheville Police Department. I was on patrol and saw you laying there. What happened?"

"Where were you a few minutes ago? I had just come out of a meeting at the Coxe Ave Brewery and was about to get in my car when a couple of guys came up behind me and hit me over the head. Then they used my back and ribs as a punching bag when I wouldn't answer their questions. They were behind me the entire time, so I never saw them."

"Let's go downtown and fill out a report. After the DUI fatality the other night we are keeping a close eye on anything that happens downtown, especially around the breweries." Officer Clark helped Ricky up and made sure he was ok to drive. "Follow me."

It wasn't too far to the police station. On the way Ricky called Susan to let her know what happened.

"You got your ass kicked?" she asked.

"I'm ok, thanks for asking," was his response.

"You'll be fine," she said.

"How do you know when you haven't even seen me? Anyway, we might need some help on this one. I think we need someone to watch our backs. I'll call you when I'm done with the police." Click.

Ricky found a parking space next to the police department. After he parked, he walked around to the front of the building where Officer Cark was waiting for him.

They went inside, got Ricky a visitors' badge, and within a few minutes he was seated at a desk ready to give his statement. With Officer Clark sitting directly across from him, Ricky went over the afternoon's events again. On the third time through, the double doors leading to the boiler room, as the officers referred to it, swung open and in came Lt. Dan Dalton. Ricky heard him before he saw him. He was barking orders and getting the officers hopping. Lt. Dalton stopped at the desk where Ricky sat. "Who are you?" he barked.

"Well like I told the last guy who asked that, I'm Peter Pan, who the hell are you?"

"You might want to check that attitude. I'm Lt. Dan Dalton. What are you doing downtown?"

"I didn't know I needed police permission to go downtown," Ricky said. "Look, I'm a private investigator and I was coming out of a meeting at the Coxe Ave Brewery when two clowns jumped me and used me for their daily workout. Gym memberships must be really expensive in this town."

"Do you need to go to the hospital?" Lt. Dalton asked.

"Are they as pleasant as you? No, I don't need the hospital," Ricky said.

"PI huh? Who are you working for?" Lt. Dalton snapped back.

"Private Investigator, and I can't reveal who my client is."

"OK. You need to understand, I have a mess going on with the death of the landscaper the other night and the brewery vandalism. Things are tense around here. Then we find you unconscious across the street from the same brewery where it all started with blood running down your neck. I don't have time for your bullshit, so just answer the questions."

"Is there blood on my shirt? Damn this my favorite shirt, how much blood is on it?" Ricky said, stalling. "Is my hat ok?" he asked, grabbing it for a quick look. "You already know I'm not going to reveal who my clients are, it's bad for business."

Lt. Dalton had enough. "I'm tired of you $200 a day guys coming in here with your crappy attitudes."

"Plus expenses," Ricky snapped back.

"What did you just say?" Dalton said spinning to ensure Ricky saw his glare.

"You mean, $200 a day plus expenses. That was in 1974 so you might want to catch up on the times."

"OUT! Get out of my police station," Dalton yelled. "If I see you anywhere near anything, I'm running you in and throwing you in jail. I'll figure out the charges when I feel like it. OUT!"

Ricky stood to leave and started walking out. He turned his head toward Lt. Dalton. "Nice town you have here Dalton. I assume you work for the Chamber of Commerce as well."

Officer Clark hurried Ricky along, took his visitor badge at the door, and made sure he left the building.

Standing outside the door of the police station, Ricky thought he would cross the street and have a beer at Pack Tavern and process what just happened. He changed his mind and went to Pack Square and found a bench to get some fresh air. His head still hurt. More importantly, he was further away from the police department in case Lt. Dalton or Officer Clark decided they wanted to talk to him more.

Sitting on a bench that faced an amphitheater, he mentally walked through the entire afternoon. How did those guys know he had been meeting with the brewery owners? It told him one important thing. Someone was keeping an eye on the brewery where the New Yorkers were drinking before the accident. After walking through it a second time, he decided he wanted some back up. He sent a simple two-word email, then he called Susan to let her know he was done with the police and would be back at the Inn within the hour.

At the same time Ricky sent his email, Jimmy received a text. "The guy you roughed up this morning is a PI named Ricky Temple. He wouldn't say who he worked for, but odds are it's the breweries. You might want to keep an eye on him if you're planning anything else."

Phil Bradley walked into Frank's Roman Pizza and saw Bobbi already sitting at their usual table. Phil was from the small city of Palm Coast, Florida just south of Port St. Lucie. He served on the town council for four terms but when his wife passed away, he decided he wanted a change of scenery. Asheville was on the top of his list after spending a long weekend there with her shortly before she died. It doesn't hurt that Asheville has all four seasons and the humidity in summer is low.

The waiter had already put his unsweetened iced tea at his place. "Sorry I had to change lunch from Wednesday, but I have a campaign meeting, and I think it's going to take longer than I thought."

"No problem," Bobbi said. "I know technically we could be running against each other this election, but we worked well together so I wanted to keep doing these lunches. That tourism economic report will be coming out in a couple of weeks. I think we should have a joint press conference to announce it and show how much tourism has done not only for the city but the entire region," Bobbi said.

Bobbi Carnes moved to North Carolina from Salinas, California and came from money. In her younger years she hitchhiked around the US and after a couple of years of seeing the country, she landed in Salinas. She gave back to her community by serving on the City Council for three terms. Salinas liked her but she got bored, and Salinas let her slip away. She moved to Asheville after selling her house. Bobbi arrived in town with money to spend and paid several hundred thousand dollars over the asking price.

"I think that's a good idea if the numbers are good. Which they should be after all the money we told the Chamber of Commerce and Visit Asheville to put into the new marketing campaign. This is a tourist town, and we need to keep the tourists that are already coming and attract more first-time visitors," Phil said as their pizza arrived.

When Phil Bradley left his lunch meeting with Bobbi Carnes, he drove the 55 minutes south to Hendersonville, NC for his next appointment. He found a parking place in a bank parking lot then walked into the Tavern. He went to a table in the back corner, as had been agreed on for their initial meeting. The person he was meeting with was waiting.

"I don't want to be here long. I don't want to be seen. Can we get to the point?" Phil Bradley said.

"If you didn't want to be spotted then you shouldn't have worn that bright red flowered shirt. You stick out already," he said.

"Ok, Ok. What we are proposing is this: for an agreed amount of money you will make sure you get me votes from business owners downtown. When I'm elected, I will use my seat to push a big increase in tourism dollars and will try to get city functions at your brewery," Phil started off.

"Initially, you will be sliding an envelope to me to get the votes. After you're elected, I will slide an envelope to you to use your influence to get what I want?" the brewery owner said.

"As odd as that sounds, yes," Phil said.

"One more thing for you, some of the owners have hired a PI to find out who is messing with us. I'll keep you informed. I want to make sure you keep the focus on tourism. We need all we can get," he said.

"Do we have an agreement? How's business after the local died in the accident?" Phil asked.

"We have an agreement. I've had a slight drop off but nothing terrible yet." He didn't want to linger too long either.

Phil stood up and extended his hand to his new partner. The two shook and Phil waited for the brewery owner to leave before he headed back to work.

Chapter 5

Six miles South of Wynot, Nebraska, down a dirt road sits the farm RJ Floyd has been working as a second career. He has been raising cattle for the last seven years and now has a hundred head. Like all farmers, he gets up early every morning to start his day and today is no different. It was already cold in northeast Nebraska and snow was in the forecast for next week, it was early this year. He was moving quickly today because he had a veteran's group meeting this evening. His wife, Money as everyone called her, made some coffee and bacon and eggs for his breakfast as she does every morning. RJ and Money have been married for 25 years and met when RJ was stationed in Korea during his early days in the Army. A smartass buddy at The Command had given her the nickname Money because he couldn't pronounce her name.

He reminded her about his meeting and headed out to start his daily chores. He really didn't feel like working all day and then going to the meeting, but he had no choice. RJ was the post commander for going on three years and wished someone else would take over. But he enjoyed it and helping veterans was an important part of his life. They had always planned on going back to Nebraska when he retired from the military, and it didn't take the two of them long to fall in love with the country life. He worked hard, six days a week, sometimes seven, but Saturdays in the fall were for Cornhusker football. There is no bigger fan than RJ Floyd. His Cornhuskers are playing Iowa on Saturday but instead of thinking about the game, he was thinking about the recent coaching change. He didn't think it was the best coaching hire, but he was willing to give it a shot. It's not like he wasn't going to watch the game.

By 11:30, it was still cold outside, and RJ was hungry. He jumped out of the truck and went into the house to get a sandwich and warm up before he started his afternoon chores. As he walked in, Money stopped what she was doing and gave him a look.

"What? I took out the trash," RJ said as he got the sandwich stuff out of the refrigerator. He grabbed a New Belgium 1554 beer as well. The beauty of working for himself was if he wanted a beer, he could have one.

"You got an email from Ricky Temple. It's only two words."

RJ stopped what he was doing and stared at her. "What are the two words?"

"Help Asheville," she told him. Money knew what was coming next.

RJ and Ricky had first met many years ago on a deployment to Afghanistan when they were working out of a safe house in Kabul. Throughout the deployment they had a few close calls which brought them closer and soon they were inseparable. When they got back, they took desk jobs to cool off for a bit. Soon they were having beers after work and took turns having each other over for cookouts on the weekends. When Ricky and Susan got married, RJ served as his best man and then the four of them became close. When it was time to retire, RJ went first and a couple of years later Ricky followed. They've looked after each other ever since and helped each other through all the issues retiring from the military brings.

He got emails like this on occasion and knew Ricky only sent them when he really needed his help. Either of them would drop everything to help their old friend. Just as now RJ would be heading to Asheville.

"Where is my bag, and gear cases?" RJ asked. Like Ricky, he keeps large plastic cases filled with trail cameras, listening devices, radios, tracking tags, and ammo for situations just like this.

"I had a feeling you would want to leave right away. Everything is by the door except your cases of equipment, and you know where all those are. You might want to double check what's in there, but it should be close," she said.

"Call Dad to help with the farm while I'm gone. If you need to, call Leo next door, he's always willing to help. Not sure what Ricky's got himself into, so I have no idea when I'll be back. As soon as I get the run down from him, I'll let you know."

With that, RJ loaded his truck, gave Money a kiss, and started down the driveway. He worked his way to Highway 12 East which would eventually take him south of Sioux City, Iowa where he would pick up I-29 and start his trip south. It would be a long trip to the mountains of North Carolina.

Jimmy called Billy after he got the text about this Ricky Temple guy. They decided to meet at McDonald's to talk about the new developments. They ordered food and sat in Jimmy's truck to talk in private. Jimmy showed Billy the text and they decided that one of them needed to try to keep an eye on Ricky Temple. They agreed to meet at Billy's house after work to discuss this new wrinkle and start a plan for the warehouse. Ronnie needed to be there as well.

Ronnie got to Billy's house around 7:00 and was the last to arrive. Jimmy filled him in on everything that had happened during the day. He wasn't too happy that Jimmy beat up this guy but knew it was more frustration from the loss of their good friend. Still, taking that chance was not a good idea, especially in daylight.

"I think we are ready to hit that warehouse. Send a message," Jimmy said, moving on to a new topic. "We need to keep hurting them and the only thing they care about is their bank accounts."

"Tell me again which breweries own this warehouse?" Ronnie asked.

"Coxe Ave Brewing, which is where the two Yankees were drinking before murdering Dave, Asheville Beer Facility, and

Circus Act Brewery," Jimmy reminded him. "We hit it on Wednesday night, the day after the City Council meeting. The plan is to destroy all the supplies. We'll go just after midnight so nobody should be there. We want to hit their finances, not hurt anyone. As for the City Council meeting, I'll take that one. I know you have your own plan for the meeting. It will be our coming out party," Jimmy laughed.

"Ok, I got it. I think we plan for now but hold off. Let's see how everything else develops," Ronnie said. "When we do move forward, I think we should do something else a few hours before the warehouse fire. A distraction downtown. I know Bobby will ensure nobody is near the warehouse, but a distraction will draw the attention of the media and the police away from where you guys are."

"I like it. We have been talking about breaking some windows or something like that. This seems like a great time to try it. I'll plan it with some of our friends," Billy said. "Are you good with this, Jimmy?"

"Hell yeah I am. I think we should move forward now but I see your point." Jimmy said.

The three remaining members of the Boys put business aside the rest of the night. Daves memorial service was at 9:00 the next morning. It was decided Billy would pick Sara up at 8:00. They would meet everyone at a grocery store in Weaverville and then drive to the service together. He would take her back home when it was over. After the service, Sara and the Boys would be at the house so people could drop by for one last visit before trying to get back to normal. When the open house was over, Billy would try to find the PI and Jimmy would drive by the warehouse that sits beside the French Broad River.

Ricky sat straight up in bed. He couldn't breathe. All he kept thinking was it was too dark. It's too dark in here. He kept looking around for some sort of light. Susan realized Ricky was having one of his dreams and got out of bed. She cracked the door to the bathroom and turned on the light. When she got back to bed, she gently rubbed his back to try to help calm him down.

Ricky looked at the clock. It was 10:42. They always seemed to happen before midnight. The dreams had been going on for years with no real pattern. Ricky sat there for just over an hour staring at the light from the bathroom. This was a bad one and he was afraid to close his eyes again. He finally fell asleep a little after midnight.

Thursday morning, Ricky and Susan again went to The Sunset Terrace for morning coffee. Although the view didn't change, they wanted to see the beauty of the early morning mountains one last time. More importantly, it was calming for Ricky after a rough night. It was their final day at the Inn and as soon as they finished with coffee they would need to pack up and get over to the rental house a few miles away.

When they got back to their room, Susan turned on the TV to catch the end of the morning news. WAVL was reporting on the funeral services for Dave Finley. Ricky called the front desk and asked for the car to be brought up at 10:00 and then helped Susan pack up.

Susan and Ricky put the final things in the car and checked out of The Grove Park Inn, ending their luxury stay. Ricky drove to the exit and took a right.

Billy finished putting on his tie and grabbed the keys to his Bronco. He left for the funeral a few minutes early to make sure he was on time to pick up Sara. After meeting the others, the two cars drove the short distance to Lake Louise Park. Ronnie had called in a favor from a friend on the Weaverville Town Council and they were nice enough to let them use the park for Dave's memorial service.

As they turned onto Lake Louise Drive, they were shocked that the road was nearly blocked with cars. People streamed into the park from all sides. They all thought they would be the only ones there.

Someone tapped on Billy's window and told him two spots had been saved for them near the Weaverville Community Center. He thanked them and the two cars made their way over to the saved spots. Sara was in tears when she realized all these people were there for Dave.

The four of them made their way past the playground to the pavilion where they intended to hold the ceremony. Ronnie guessed there were over 300 people there. He was in shock.

"We are with you, Sara Dunn," one person said as they walked by.

"Anything you need, Sara, you just ask," another said.

Ronnie stood on top of a picnic table and looked around before he started talking into the megaphone he was handed. "We are overwhelmed by this support. Dave Finley was a good man. He was out trying to make a living for himself and to support his fiancée, Sara. He worked hard and was always a good friend. He loved this city. He grew up here and came back to start his business with Jimmy. What happened was senseless. We still don't understand. The three of us, as well as the community, now have a void that can't be filled. We will never forget all of you that came out here today. Remember what happened, how it happened, ask yourself why this happened. But most importantly remember Dave Finley."

Ronnie stepped down from the table, dropped his head, and broke down. As he started to cry, he felt Sara's arms wrapped around him, then Jimmy's and finally Billy's. When Ronnie tried to end the hug, he was surprised he couldn't. It wasn't just the four of them but everyone there had joined in with them, becoming one big community hug for Dave.

After playing some of Dave's favorite songs, including D'yer Mak'er at Sara's request, they walked back to their cars. It was a short ceremony, but it was all they could handle. The support continued as they walked through those gathered.

"We can't let this be forgotten," yelled one lady.

"Asheville needs to get under better control," said an older man.

It took some time, but Billy got Sara back to her house. After the open house that lasted a few hours, he drove home to change clothes before picking up Jimmy to go back downtown to try to find Ricky Temple. He was more determined than ever.

Driving past the WAVL studios, Ricky headed down Macon Avenue. "This afternoon, I'm going to see the other breweries and take a walk around. I didn't get a good feel for downtown the other day. I'm hoping if someone is actually watching the breweries, I can flush them out. Have you gotten any more info yet on the Dave Finley accident?" he asked Susan.

"I have some, but there are a few more things I want to check out. I should have something for you when you get back. Are you feeling any better after getting kicked around a few days ago and after last night?"

"You are really enjoying my pain, aren't you?"

"You'll be fine," she said. This was her usual response when Ricky was hurt. She noticed he didn't bring up his dream last night.

As they got to the bottom of Sunset Mountain, Ricky waited at the stop sign for his GPS to direct him. After a couple of quick turns, they turned right on to Kimberly Avenue. Ricky realized he was on the street he could see from the Sunset Terrace.

"These houses are beautiful. What a great neighborhood." Susan said.

"No kidding, I'm sure we could never afford anything around here. I wonder what the price comparison is for these houses now versus 25 or 30 years ago?" he said.

He was starting to remember the area. Ricky was giving himself a hard time, mentally, for not realizing how much of Asheville he had forgotten. He remembered to stay on Kimberly and turn on the road that ran beside his elementary school then down the steep hill to Merrimon Avenue. No need for GPS now, he thought.

"I can't get over how narrow these streets are. Lots of cars on the road," Susan said. "I forgot to tell you, I got a text from Father Tim. He said he had been busy helping a family in his Parrish but wants to meet later today at the place where you two used to hang out. It's his day off so he said to just text him when we are free, and he'll be there."

As Ricky pulled up to the traffic light at Merrimon Avenue, he said, "Sounds good. If you look to the left, on the other side of the gas station you will see Mitchell's Sports Bar which is where Tim and I used to hang out. Across the street is where the Winn-Dixie and Roses used to be. Looks like a Stein Mart and Sav-Mor Foods is there now."

The city was coming back to Ricky more and more now. After turning onto Merrimon Avenue the car fell quiet. It wasn't too much further to the rental house. After passing Beaver Lake they turned where their GPS directed them. They continued around the sharp and narrow right-hand curve and then eventually up the steep hill to Graystone Road. It was 10:20 when they pulled into their rental house on the quiet dead-end street.

He pulled into the garage and immediately shut the door. No need for people to see more than they needed. They entered the house through the door in the garage which led directly to the kitchen. The kitchen led to the dining room and then a living room on the left and a hallway leading to three bedrooms and two bathrooms. They decided they would use the first bedroom on the left as an office for Susan, and they would sleep in the main bedroom on the right at the end of the hall.

After unpacking, Ricky asked Susan to print out a map of greater Asheville and a map of just downtown.

"Can we eat first?" she asked. "I'm hungry."

"Sure, do you want to order or go somewhere? It makes no difference to me."

"Let's just order, you know how I am. I can't relax until I'm set up. Now, I have an assignment to worry about too."

When lunch arrived, they decided to eat by the firepit in the backyard. Although it was cloudy, it was still a great day to sit outside. When they finished eating, Ricky laid down on the sofa to get some rest before heading downtown. He didn't get much sleep with all the noise coming from the office. Around 12:45 the office went quiet. He thought he would get a solid fifteen minutes of rest before heading out. Then the printer started. He assumed it was the maps he wanted.

When the printer stopped, Ricky went into the office to see the maps. He showed Susan the three main routes from the rental house to downtown. The first is the way they had already driven, which went down Charlotte Street and brought them downtown from the east. The second is to go straight down Merrimon Avenue which had a lot of stop lights, but it dropped you right in the middle of town. The third, and probably the quickest, was on the highway and would bring them in on the west side. He asked her to mark each one using a different color.

"Thanks for printing those. They look good. I'm heading out now. Will you text Tim and see if he can meet us around three?" he yelled toward the office.

"I got it. Be careful this time," was the response.

Ricky decided to take the Merrimon Avenue route. During the drive he got a text from Susan letting him know Tim would meet them at 3:00. Tim would pick up Susan since he was only a few minutes away. Ricky went from Merrimon Avenue to Broadway Street to Biltmore Avenue without ever turning, as it is just one long street.

He pulled into a parking garage and found an empty spot. His first stop would be the Asheville Beer Facility, a short walk down Biltmore Avenue. As he entered, he immediately noticed how different it was from the Coxe Ave Brewery. Asheville Beer Facility was more modern, whereas Coxe Ave was more rustic. Like Coxe Ave Brewery, Asheville Beer Facility had a large garage door to open during good weather. Ricky thought the garage door thing must be the formula here. Today the door was shut as it was getting cooler and cloudy with a chance of rain later.

Ricky decided to sit at the bar. He walked across the concrete floor to the metal bar and uncomfortable-looking metal bar stools. He knew he wouldn't linger because his back wouldn't be able to handle sitting on those stools for very long. From the other end of the bar, the young 20-something bartender walked over to where Ricky was sitting and placed a Miller High Life in front of him. Ricky must have had a confused look on his face because she simply pointed to the opposite side of the taproom. Ricky turned and saw Mike Lamb standing there. He nodded at Ricky and went about his business.

"What's your name?" Ricky asked.

JoJo was the short direct response. Ricky noticed the tattoos on her arm and her multiple piercings. JoJo had no intention of hanging around to talk to him.

"Are you from Asheville?" he asked.

"Yeah, I was born here. Just never left. Let me know if you want another beer. Mike said to take care of you." With that, JoJo moved on to another customer.

As a Tom Petty song started playing overhead, Ricky got up and walked around but wasn't sure what he was looking for. The place was about a quarter full, which he thought was light for an early Thursday afternoon. He imagined it would slowly pick up as the evening arrived and then be full by the time Thursday night football started.

He finished his beer and signaled JoJo for another. "How much do I owe you?" Ricky asked her.

"No idea, nobody has ever had that beer in here. I'll check and be right back." She told him. "Looks like you owe me a whopping $5," she said dryly when she got back from talking to Mike Lamb. He paid for the beers and thanked her. Ricky quickly drank his beer then headed for the door.

As soon as he stepped outside, he felt it. Somone was behind him, but Ricky needed to be sure he wasn't imagining things. He walked up Biltmore Avenue toward the parking garage. As he got to the entrance to a hotel, he turned left and walked down the short but steep hill of Aston Street. The person stayed about 10 feet behind him. Ricky got to the bottom of the hill and stopped at a wine bar that was closed. All he wanted was the reflection in the window so he could get a look at the guy. He got a quick glimpse of a stocky guy with a beard and a green trucker hat. Ricky turned and walked back up the hill as the green hat guy ducked into the hotel's parking garage. He was sure the guy was following him now. He wanted to be ahead of him this time, assuming it was the same guy from the parking lot a few days earlier. At the top of the hill, Ricky crossed Biltmore Avenue and went into a coffee shop.

"I'll have a medium black coffee and cinnamon roll," he told the guy working the counter. As he waited, Ricky scanned the restaurant. The green hat guy was outside but still on the other side of the street. He was keeping an eye on the front door. Behind Ricky in line was a short very skinny guy wearing a local baseball team hat and sunglasses.

"Could there be two of them?" Ricky thought as he got his order and took a seat. Something about the sunglasses guy didn't feel right either. As usual, he wanted a table where he could see the door as well as the inside of the café. He decided to test his theory.

Ricky saw someone sitting on the other side of the café reading a newspaper. He got up and walked over.

"Excuse me, if you're done with the business section do you mind if I borrow it?" he asked. The guy handed him the business section and Ricky turned to see the sunglasses guy watching him. So, there were two of them.

Ricky checked his watch. It was about 2:10. He had to meet Susan and Tim soon, so he ate his cinnamon roll, took his coffee, and headed for the door. He got back to his car, got in, and cranked the radio – some metal this time. His adrenaline was starting to pump, and he was happy to be on offense.

Ricky pulled out of the parking garage and went right. As soon as he was on Biltmore Avenue, he saw a white Ford Bronco behind him. He went a couple of blocks to the middle of town and turned right again, he wanted to see if the Bronco was following him. When the Bronco turned to stay behind him, he decided taking the Charlotte Street route back towards the house would be best. The streets in downtown Asheville were one big choke point. Narrow and one way, people just crossed the street whenever and wherever they wanted. Cars were only sort of in parking spaces. Not ideal for this kind of thing. Ricky was yelling in frustration the entire time.

Ricky realized he was in a slow speed pursuit. 'It must be a white Bronco thing,' he thought. At Charlotte Street, he went left heading north. He had already picked the spot where he wanted to confront them if they stayed with him. As he crossed over I-240 and started up the hill his frustration with the traffic was getting the best of him. He decided to get off Charlotte Street and see if the Merrimon Avenue route was better. Ricky went left at the stoplight by Fuddruckers Hamburgers, which he immediately regretted because it was even more narrow. Cars were parked on the street turning a two-lane road into one. He made it to Merrimon Avenue and went right heading for North Asheville. The Bronco kept coming. They either didn't care that Ricky knew they were back there, or they just weren't good at this.

"Keep with me. Come on, keep with me a few more miles and then let's see what you are going to do," Ricky said. The two cars continued up Merrimon Avenue. They passed an elementary school, and then a few minutes later they passed the park where Ricky had played little league baseball as a kid.

"Keep with me, come on," Ricky yelled as they passed the post office and McDonald's. He was almost at the turn he wanted. His adrenaline was flowing now. He went down the hill by the liquor store and got into the lane to turn left into the old Roses parking lot. The light was green, so he didn't have to wait. The Bronco came with him, and Ricky grinned because he knew had them where he wanted them.

As Ricky and the Bronco came up the entrance to the parking lot, he saw what he was looking for in the back of the parking lot under a tree. When he got to the entrance Ricky suddenly sped up, making a fast right turn and then a sharp right into the empty parking lot. His car spun around so it was making a "T" with the Bronco as it came around the corner. As they approached Ricky's car, they hit their brakes not seeing the red Ford Raptor speeding up from behind them. The Raptor headed for the front of the Bronco and stopped a foot short. At the same time, Ricky and the Raptor driver jumped out ready for whatever happened next. The Bronco reversed and sped off, going around the Raptor, down the hill towards the grocery store.

Ricky looked over with a big smile and said, "RJ, brother, it's good to see you."

"You too brother. I had no idea what was going on when you came into the café and didn't even wave hello. But when you came over and asked for the newspaper and then looked at the guy with the sunglasses, I figured it out. I already had the guy outside with the green hat. He was obvious. Man, the congestion in downtown Asheville is nothing more than a choke point. When you sent the address of the intercept, I peeled off to get here. It sucked. And what's with you suddenly reading the business page? Hell, I had no idea you could read at all," RJ said, laughing.

"Let's get out of here. We don't need to attract any more attention. Before we meet up with the others, I had another dream last night. It woke me up around 10:30," Ricky said.

"Are you ok? How often are you having them?" RJ asked.

"Last night was the first time in a couple of months. I think I'm good," Ricky said.

"We'll talk later," RJ said.

"I'm glad you're here. Susan will be happy to see you, too. We're heading across the street to that bar," Ricky said while pointing at Mitchell's Sports Bar. "We'll probably avoid being seen together for a few days. It will give you better freedom of movement, but we are ok in this place. It will make more sense after I tell you the situation. Susan is already there with another guy you need to meet."

The two cars drove across the street. As Ricky parked, he noticed a police car driving through the parking lot they had just left. Something seemed odd about it, but he just registered it in the back of his mind for later and joined the others inside.

"Look who I found!" Ricky exclaimed as he and RJ walked in. Susan jumped up and gave RJ a long hug. She was excited to see their old friend. It had been a few years.

"Oh yeah, well look who I found," Susan said as she pointed to Father Tim. Susan introduced Father Tim and RJ.

This time it was Ricky giving the long hug. He was always happy to see Tim, and it had been way too long.

"This place reminds me of that bar up in Freeport, Maine we went to when we were working up there. How did you find it?" asked RJ.

Father Tim answered. "After Ricky and I graduated from college, we both came home for a few years. This was our hang out. The funny thing is, we used to come here to watch the Charlotte Hornets play. It is a sports bar after all. We would come in here to watch games, but they would never be able to find them on TV. So, we would come in and have beers and ask the staff over and over to put sports on. It turned into our little game."

As Father Tim finished his story, the waitress arrived to take drink orders. It was the usual all the way around: Ricky had his Miller High Life; Susan got a Chablis; RJ had 1554; and Father Tim asked for the Circus Act stout. As the waitress walked away, Ricky asked her to put the Red Sox game on. Everyone at the table laughed.

"RJ, did Ricky tell you he got his ass kicked the other day?" Susan asked.

"No, but now might be a good time to fill me in on what the deal is. You getting your ass kicked doesn't sound like the beginning."

For the next 30 minutes, Ricky and Susan told Father Tim and RJ everything that had happened since they got the phone call in Kill Devil Hills. Father Tim filled in the parts he knew and now everyone had some idea of the situation.

"Do you think the guys that just followed you are the same ones from the parking lot the other day?" RJ asked.

"Not sure, but that would make sense," Ricky said.

Ricky told RJ and Father Tim about the rental house they were using as their base. They decided Father Tim would go about his business keeping his ears open. RJ would get a rental car in the morning and switch it out every week and Ricky would do the same. RJ and Ricky gave Susan a description of the Bronco and the license plate number.

Susan said, "I have been looking into Dave Finley. He's the one that was killed by the drunk driver last weekend," she said for RJ's benefit. "Not a lot to tell. He went to Western Carolina University, so it makes sense that he had to have some friends and some roommates. I'm going to dig into that next. He started a landscaping business with Jimmy O'Brien who also went to Western Carolina. Looks like it's been very successful. Finley was engaged to Sara Dunn, and they lived together near Weaverville which is just a few miles north of Asheville. Not much else right now. I'm going to expand my search to investigate the business partner, Jimmy O'Brien. I also need to get the name of the third friend. I found an apartment lease that mentions three roommates, but no names."

"RJ, when we get to the house, we need to set up cameras. Mainly for the front and back yards. You'll see it sits at the base of the mountain and the backyard backs up to a wooded area. It might make a good surveillance spot if anyone were to find out where we are. It's a quiet area, so the cameras in the front will tell us if any new cars have started going up and down the street. You park in the garage to keep your truck out of sight, especially after the incident a few minutes ago," Ricky said. "Did you bring all your gear?"

"Yeah, I brought everything not knowing what we needed," RJ said.

"I took a walk while you were downtown. The neighborhood is quiet, with several elderly people and a few families. I took note of some of the cars I saw and wrote them down on the board in the office," Susan offered.

"Good. Tomorrow I'm going to get a few burner phones while RJ gets his rental," Ricky said. "I'll get you one, Tim."

"One more thing for you guys," Father Tim said. "Tuesday night there is a City Council meeting. I'm hearing rumblings that there might be some fireworks. More than the usual number of locals are going, and Dave Finley's death has them fired up. Might be a good idea for you guys to be there."

"Good info, RJ and I will be there." Ricky turned toward RJ, "We both go but separately then compare notes, the usual stuff. Maybe green hat or sunglasses guy will be there."

Father Tim had walked over to the bar and yelled back towards the table, "Ricky, come over here. I want you to meet someone. This is Kenny King. He owns the place now," Father Tim said as Ricky got up to walk over to the bar where Tim was standing. "He's agreed to keep a running tab for us while you are in town."

"Kenny King, nice to meet you. Just call me Ricky T. If you have plenty of Miller High Life we will get along great," Ricky said.

"Let me know what you need," Kenny said as they all started walking toward the door.

"That guy is going to be trouble. Ronnie is going to be pissed with us getting sucked in like that," Billy said as they sped down Lakeshore Drive towards safety.

"Hell, I'm pissed we got sucked in like that," Jimmy added.

Billy's phone buzzed. A new text.

"Got a text from Bobby. He said nobody was in that parking lot when he went through," Billy said. "We need get a handle on Ricky and this new guy in town. Maybe Bobby can help."

Chapter 6

Carrying three cases of Busch Light, a bag of chips, and a frozen pizza, Billy kicked open the door to the basement.

"What's wrong with you?" Ronnie said, sitting in his chair drinking the last beer in the fridge. He was proud of himself for being early for a change. So, he didn't mind taking the last one.

"I stopped at the store to stock up on beer. I was about to pull into a parking space when some little miss thing in a Mercedes SUV with Ohio license plates cut me off. Then she jumps out, looks at me and grins as she walks into the store!" Billy yelled. "Plus, the beer was almost $18 a case."

"That's exactly what is ruining our town and why we are doing what we are doing," Jimmy said. "How about passing around some of those beers?" The others noticed Jimmy had been much quieter since Dave's memorial service. "Just so you guys know, I'll have to go do some work tomorrow, I can't hold it off any longer."

"Billy, are you mad at the idiot driver or are you mad about Dave?" Ronnie asked.

"Both!" he yelled back at Ronnie. "Dave is dead. In fact, let's remember he was murdered. I'm tired of everyone saying it was an accident."

"Don't you see, Jimmy is right. That is why we are doing everything we are doing. We need these tourists gone so we can reclaim our city. We've been dealing with idiots like you just saw in the parking lot for a long time. Try to calm down and keep your head screwed on. This is no time to lose control," Ronnie advised.

"You're right. Maybe it was bad timing since we just had the memorial," Billy said.

After Billy calmed down, they filled Ronnie in on the slow speed chase. For the next hour, the three of them talked through the plan for the City Council meeting on Tuesday and continued to plan the warehouse attack for Wednesday night.

Sitting around the fire pit, Ricky, Susan, and RJ caught up on old times. It had been a long day setting up security cameras and testing out the equipment RJ brought. They decided that tomorrow RJ would drive around and get familiar with the city, while Susan tried to track down the Bronco and get the name and address of the owner.

"I found something today that might be important," Susan said, "A guy named Ronnie Jenkins is running for City Council. He registered to get his name on the ballot and hasn't done any campaigning since. Other than the two incumbents, he and another local named Nick Zika are the only ones running. He owns a restaurant in South Asheville called Pappas Greek Table. It's very popular. He is making some appearances around town."

"So, what's the connection?" Ricky asked.

"Turns out, Ronnie Jenkins was a college roommate of Dave Finley. I found an apartment lease with their names on it out near the school they went to," Susan said. "He is having his first rally on Saturday. He is the manager of one of the banks downtown. After what Father Tim told us, I thought it might be too much of a coincidence that they were roommates and now he's cranking up his campaign. Especially after Dave Finley was killed." Susan took a sip of her Chablis. "As for Nick Zika, I don't see any connection other than he is a local, born and raised here."

"Good point," said Ricky. "Susan, you and RJ go to the Jenkins rally. RJ, you provide cover for her. We don't know if the green hat guy or sunglasses guy will be there. Hell, for all we know this Ronnie Jenkins could be one of the guys from the Bronco."

"Well, take a look," Susan said. "This is his picture from the bank website. Does he look familiar?"

"No, that's not one of our guys. You agree RJ?" Ricky asked. RJ nodded in agreement.

"Ok, to be on the safe side, here is a picture of Zika. Does he look familiar?" Susan said.

"Actually yes. I think I might have gone to high school with him but no, he wasn't in the Bronco," Ricky said.

"Agree it's neither of them. Susan, I'll drive us downtown and drop you off a few blocks away, then park. I'll come from the opposite direction from where I drop you off. Don't acknowledge me. We both need to use our phones to take pictures. When it's over I'll pick you up at the same spot I dropped you off. How does that sound?"

All agreed on the plan. RJ would drive the route after he picked up a rental car in the morning. Susan would get an Uber to the store to restock the house. While all this was going on, Ricky would check out the bank where Ronnie Jenkins worked.

The next morning, Susan got an Uber to the store and picked up house supplies, which consisted mostly of snacks and Chablis. On her way back to the house she was thinking about how much more things cost but she knew it was the cost of doing business. She came home from the store to find a white truck with a trailer in front of the house. As she got out of the Uber, a short skinny guy with sunglasses came up to her.

"Hey ma'am, I'm Jimmy O'Brien. My landscaping business has a contract to cut the grass and take care of the leaves for this rental house. You know all the stuff for this time of year. We'll be out of here in about an hour. How long will you be using the house?"

Susan froze when she heard the name Jimmy O'Brien. She recognized him from her research, not only as Dave Finley's business partner but also as a friend of Ronnie Jenkins. Her mind was racing. Was this a coincidence or did he know who had rented the house?

Susan calmed herself down and regrouped. "Hi, I'm Susan Gilmore," she said, using her maiden name. She wasn't sure if he would recognize the last name of Temple since she didn't know what his connection to everything was, if any. She realized Jimmy O'Brien fit the description of one of the guys from the slow car chase a couple of days earlier. "I'll be here a few more weeks. I'm from Kill Devil Hills and needed a break from the beach life."

"Ok, hope you have a good visit. I'll be back next Friday for more leaves," Jimmy said as he walked away.

Susan looked at the name on the side of the truck, Cats Landscaping. It had a phone number and website listed. She hurried into the house putting her groceries down in the kitchen and then went straight to the office. She dialed Ricky's number while she pulled up the website.

"Where are you?" she asked.

"I'm downtown walking around the bank. What's going on? You sound off."

"I just met Dave Finley's business partner, Jimmy O'Brien. They have the landscaping contract for this house. I'm on their website now and I'm going to send you a picture. The guy I saw fit your description of one of the Bronco guys. Short, very skinny, wearing a baseball hat and sunglasses," Susan said. She was talking very fast. She wasn't used to coming face-to-face with someone they were investigating.

"Hold on, I'm bringing RJ in on this call," Ricky said.

"Just got the picture you sent. Yep, that's one of the guys from the other day," Ricky said. RJ agreed.

"RJ let's get to the house. I want to look at the camera footage to make sure he wasn't nosing around the garage and spotted your truck. He would have recognized it from the parking lot. Then let's go over what we know," Ricky said.

Forty-five minutes later everyone was at the house. While she waited for the guys, Susan printed out pictures of Dave Finley and Jimmy O'Brien from the website. She wrote "deceased" on the bottom of the picture of Dave Finley. On the picture of Jimmy O'Brien, she wrote "sunglasses guy" below his name. Susan also printed the picture of Ronnie Jenkins and put a question mark below his name. Lastly, she had a piece of paper with a large question mark on it with "green hat guy" on the bottom. She added all the pictures to the board.

When everyone had arrived, Susan went over everything that happened that morning three times. She knew that was how Ricky worked. He was processing everything and needed to hear it all several times. RJ was listening but going over the camera footage at the same time.

"Ok, one more time but you can leave out the part about the Chablis," Ricky said.

Before she could start again, RJ said he didn't think Jimmy O'Brien was looking around and was comfortable that he hadn't seen his truck. Based on what Susan said, RJ thought Jimmy's presence was a coincidence.

Susan told the story again. "And you don't think he had any idea who you are?" Ricky asked.

"I don't. I agree with RJ. I think it's one of those weird things and they happen to have the contract to take care of the lawn here," Susan said.

"Ok. So, we know Dave Finley was killed by a drunk driver. Dave and Jimmy O'Brien own Cats Landscaping. Ronnie Jenkins is a bank manager and is running for City Council but he's running quietly. I was jumped in a parking lot but didn't see who did it. I was followed by a white Bronco with two guys in it. One we now know is Jimmy O'Brien and we don't know who the other one, green hat guy is. We know at least three of the breweries are being harassed by those who we think are locals. I think an assumption would be O'Brien and green hat guy are two of those guys," Ricky summed up. "What did I miss?"

"I think that's it for now," RJ and Susan agreed.

"Susan, find an address for Jimmy O'Brien. While you two are at the Jenkins rally tomorrow, I'll drive by O'Brien's house," Ricky said.

Billy was spending the afternoon in Hendersonville doing a few estimates for the spring. He was also using the time to put up signs for Ronnie in South Asheville when he was done with work. He went to his usual Hendersonville lunch spot and walked into the Tavern to get something to eat and a beer.

Billy was a little surprised to see Phil Bradley sitting at a table in the back corner. He is easy to spot because he always wears those bright flower shirts. They didn't know each other at all so Billy didn't think much of Bradley being there until he saw a familiar face join him at his table.

'Why is that brewery owner sitting with Bradley?' Billy thought to himself. He felt lucky that neither of them knew him, so he didn't worry too much about moving a little closer to be able to hear what they were talking about.

"Let's be quick. Money for votes and later it's money for access," Billy heard Phil Bradley say.

"That's the deal," the brewery owner replied.

Billy then saw Phil Bradley take an envelope out of the inside of his jacket and quickly slide it over to the owner. It was over very fast, so Billy didn't have time to take his phone out and take pictures.

When the crooked politician and brewery owner left, Billy decided to skip lunch and get to his truck to call the Boys.

Sitting in his truck, Billy dialed Ronnie's number first. When he answered he told him to hold on as he added Jimmy. Once he had everyone connected, he told them what he had just seen.

"I can't believe it. It was obvious the envelope had money in it. I couldn't tell how much," Billy said.

"You're sure he said he was paying him to get votes and then later he would get access?" Ronnie asked.

"That's what he said. I couldn't hear the entire conversation but I'm positive they were talking about money and votes. I moved close enough to get the key words without being obvious," Billy replied.

"What do you think, Ronnie? Do we go to the elections board or wait?" Jimmy asked.

"I think this is something we hold onto and use at the right time," Ronnie said.

"I'm pissed off enough that I vote we move our plan forward," Billy added. "I don't need any more reasons."

"We will talk about it later," Ronnie said. He didn't want to talk about the warehouse over the phone.

When Billy got back to Asheville, he met up with Jimmy in Billy's basement and started talking over the warehouse plan again. They both were mad. First Dave was killed by a drunk driver and now one of the people Ronnie was running against was buying votes and working with the owner of one of the breweries they were targeting.

"I'm going to make sure my four gas cans are filled. It won't look odd for me to do it since I need it for work. Call Sara and borrow her truck for Wednesday night. We need to remind Bobby to keep people away from the Riverside Drive warehouse, too," Jimmy said. "After the council meeting on Tuesday, I will be more recognizable. We need to keep that in mind."

"Yeah, I thought of that. I'll call Sara about the truck, no problem. It's even more important now to remember what Ronnie said. The circle is closed, we don't talk about this to anyone," Billy said.

"Man, I forgot to tell you. One of the properties we work on has this hot tourist staying at it. I talked to her for a few minutes. That's one account Trent won't be working," Jimmy laughed. "She said her name was Susan, but I don't remember the last name. Don't forget tomorrow is Ronnie's campaign thing downtown, so we need to stay away."

"I remember, I'll be watching football anyway. You aren't dropping Darby Jones for this tourist, are you?" Billy asked.

"No, you know that nobody compares to Darby. Stop by and pick me up so I don't have to drive," Jimmy told him. "What time is it? I think Darby will be on the news soon."

Saturday morning, Ricky took a Lyft to get a rental car for himself. He was careful to not use the same company as RJ. Susan found the address for Jimmy O'Brien, and she gave it to Ricky before he left. The address turned out to be a condo not far from the Asheville Country Club, an area he knew well. Ricky decided to get a coffee and cinnamon roll on the way. He texted RJ and Susan and let them know his rental car was a black Jeep Cherokee. Ricky likes as much cross talk as possible to keep everyone on the same page.

Around 10:00, RJ and Susan left the house to head for the Jenkins Rally. The rally was scheduled for 11:00 at Pritchard Park. Pritchard Park is a small triangle of green space in the middle of downtown. RJ took the highway and came downtown from the west on Patton

Avenue. His plan was to drop her at an intersection just a few blocks from the rally. She would have to walk a little, and he would turn down Ashland Avenue and circle back around to the east side of the park. RJ found a parking place beside a church and walked to the park.

As RJ approached, he saw Susan on the other side as they had arranged. He also recognized Ronnie Jenkins from the picture he had seen a few days earlier. Only about thirty people were there. RJ looked around and did not recognize anyone else. No green hat guy and no Jimmy O'Brien. He took out his phone and took a few pictures of the crowd, noting that Susan was doing the same.

Ronnie stood beside a sign with his name on it and looked at the small crowd before starting his speech. The size of the crowd didn't bother him too much, it was his first rally so if he messed up only a few people would know. Plus, he knew after Tuesday night more people would know who he was. He raised the same bullhorn from Dave's memorial service and started talking.

"I know a lot of people in this town don't know who I am or what I stand for. I have lived in Asheville my entire life and the citizens who have been here a long time do know me. It's the newcomers, the people who have lived here for only a brief time who don't know me. Some of the incumbents on the council have lived here for only a few years. That's the problem I'm addressing with my candidacy for City Council. They don't know Asheville. I know Asheville," Ronnie said emphatically to a small smattering of applause. He looked around trying to make eye contact before going on. "We need someone on the council who grew up here, whose family has been here for generations. That someone is ME. I know another local, Nick Zika is running as well and although he is a good man, he doesn't know the town the same way I do. When you elect me, I will stop handing out building permits like they are

Halloween candy. I will represent all of Asheville and not just the big hotels and breweries attracting all the tourism that has brought all the crowding to our mountain town. On November 10th vote for Ronnie Jenkins!" The applause grew a little louder but not by much.

A few minutes later, Ronnie was done. He felt good about the rally but knew he needed to practice before he spoke next time.

Ricky turned off Merrimon Avenue onto Beaverdam Road heading for Jimmy O'Brien's condo. Just past the YMCA he took a right on to Beaver Ridge Lane. He drove up the steep narrow hill. As he approached Jimmy's condo, he slammed on the brakes. Sitting in front of Jimmy's condo was a white Bronco and a guy with a green hat standing beside it. There were no parking spaces, only driveways to pull into. Ricky had no choice but to drive slowly as if he was looking for a house number to not bring attention to himself. He drove past the Bronco, careful not to stare, and then to the top of the hill by the mailboxes. He stopped the car and called RJ.

"I'm at O'Brien's house. There is a white Bronco and a guy with a green baseball hat talking to Jimmy O'Brien. I'm going to follow him but want you to change out with me and take over. Once he starts moving, I'll text you an intercept spot. Are you done with the rally?"

"Yeah, we are back at the house. We will fill you in later. Not a lot to tell, though, he was bad and obviously didn't have someone write his speech. I'll be looking for the text."

Ricky sat in his car waiting, holding his phone up to his ear as if he was on a call. Fifteen minutes later, the green hat guy and Jimmy O'Brien loaded some beer in the back and then got in the Bronco to leave. Ricky pulled out and started down the hill to follow them. He called RJ to give him a running dialogue.

"They are on the move. We just left his condo development and are heading toward Merrimon Avenue," Ricky told him.

RJ was in the office with Susan. They listened to Ricky and followed along on the maps.

"We just took a right on to Merrimon Avenue and are heading north towards Woodfin and Weaverville, in the general direction of our rental house." A few seconds later, "We just passed the North Asheville library and are approaching Beaver Lake. RJ, I need you to take over at the intersection of Stratford Road and Merrimon Avenue. If they turn before that I'll let you know."

Before RJ left, he added Susan to call so she could listen until Ricky got back to the house. RJ drove down to the end of the street, took a right, and went down the steep hill towards Merrimon Avenue. He timed it well because as he approached Merrimon Avenue, he looked left and saw the Bronco coming over the hill towards him. Ricky turned onto Stratford Road and gave RJ a slight head nod as RJ pulled in behind the Bronco and took over the surveillance.

Ricky pulled into the driveway, parked, and went straight to the office. He saw Susan had placed a pin on the map with a small picture of Jimmy O'Brien on his house. She was ready to do the same for the green hat guy if they went to his house.

"We are at the stop light at Weaverville Road waiting for the light to turn. Looks like he is going left onto a highway marked Business 19," RJ said.

Ricky was confused for a second until he studied the map. Merrimon Avenue became Weaverville Road not far from where he had turned.

"We're moving again. Turned left onto Business 19 and went under the highway, whichever it's called. Took another left onto Newbridge Parkway. Shit, they took a quick right, and I missed it."

The road RJ was on went straight into an apartment complex. He pulled into the complex and turned around, speeding up as he exited to get back to where he lost the Bronco.

"If they took a quick right, it puts them on Mills Place," Ricky said to guide RJ back into the game. "There are a couple of places they could turn left. I vote to stay on Mills Place, but you are the guy on the ground, so it's your call. If you don't see anything after a few miles, you can circle back."

"Got it and agree. I'm on Mills Place now. I'm having to drive slowly because the road is so narrow and has a lot of curves, which is helping me not stand out. There are a few houses on both sides of the street. Just took a sharp left bend in the road and now looks like a sharp right. Jackpot. I got them."

RJ relayed the address to Ricky. Susan was already on her computer, searching to find out the owner's name.

"Guess who is standing in the driveway talking to green hat and Jimmy?" RJ said. "None other than Ronnie Jenkins. That puts all three of them together, like you guessed."

After passing green hat guy's house, RJ stayed on Mills Place where he crested a hill and started back down. He came to a turnoff on the left, just before the road entered a new development up a very steep hill. It was about a quarter mile past the new target house. RJ turned around and headed back. He was careful not to slow down at the new target house but went slowly enough to get another glimpse. He saw Ronnie, Jimmy, and green hat guy walk to the back of the house to what looked like a basement entrance. RJ decided going by the house twice was enough, so he headed back to the rental house.

By the time RJ got back to the house, Susan had a name. Billy Thompson. According to a quick search, he works at a West Asheville pool company. He went to the same high school and started college with Ronnie Jenkins, Dave Finley, and Jimmy O'Brien.

"Welcome to the WAVL noon news, I'm Darby Jones. Today, the Mayor announced a $70 million project to build pickle ball courts in Asheville. The full details will be discussed at the City Council meeting on Tuesday night before they take a vote. The announcement was met with a lot of excitement around town because it will benefit both residents and tourists. If it passes the vote in the City Council, it will be on the ballot in November. Also, charges have been filed against the two tourists involved in the crash that killed Dave Finley. The driver was charged with vehicular manslaughter and driving under the influence. He could face up to 10 years in prison. More charges are expected. Last, we were at Nick Zika's campaign event this morning and will bring you the details. We'll be back after a few commercials."

"It's about time they charged that guy. I hope they fry him. And look at what the City Council thinks is important. Pickle ball? They can't be serious." Ronnie was pissed. He opened another beer and poured a shot of Jim Beam to try to calm down. "The City Council's big agenda item for Tuesday is whether to spend $70 million dollars for a park with pickle ball courts. I don't get it, we already have the French Broad River, the Appalachian Trail isn't that far, the Blue Ridge Parkway and skiing up near Boone. Now they need pickle ball courts to go along with the breweries to bring in even more tourists. Do you guys remember in the last two elections we voted on millions of dollars for new parks which raised our taxes? Now yet another new park is needed raising our taxes even more. And now we know one of them is trying to buy votes so he can continue to destroy our city."

"You sound like a candidate," Billy chided Ronnie. "What's pickle ball, anyway?"

"It's like mini tennis," Jimmy jumped in.

"I thought ping pong was mini tennis," Billy said.

"Ping pong is table tennis, and pickle ball is on an actual court just smaller than a tennis court. I am a candidate so I should sound like one," Ronnie said.

The room fell quiet as the three of them just looked at each other. After 30 seconds of silence, they all burst into loud laughter. All the tension and stress from the previous week had come to a head. It felt good to just sit there and laugh about pickle ball for a few minutes. Dave's death had taken its toll on them and the three of them didn't realize it until that moment.

"What do you think about Nick Zika?" Billy asked, bringing them back to reality.

"He's a good guy. I've met him a few times, but I will beat him. I say the rest of the night is about beer and football, we can go over the plan for the week tomorrow after the Panthers game," Ronnie said.

With nods all around and new beers passed around, the three settled into a long night of beer, football and letting the stress fade away.

Chapter 7

Ricky walked into Circus Act Brewing and searched for a seat. He wanted to make sure he went to all three of the breweries to show the owners he was with them and working. Again, he chose a seat at the bar. He looked around while he waited for the bartender to get to him. This brewery was smaller than the others and was in an old garage. There was a small bar with only a few tables around and the usual garage door that opened to a small area to stand and look out at town during good weather. Most of the space was taken up with the brewing and bottling equipment.

The young bartender walked over to Ricky and put a Miller High Life in front of him. Ricky saw the beer just as Clif Jordan walked towards him.

"Hey sport, are you the PI Clif's been talking about?" Livingston, the afternoon bartender asked.

"It's private … never mind. Yep, that's me," Ricky replied. He turned his attention to Clif.

"Did you see the noon news?' Cliff asked. "They charged the two tourists from the Dave Finley accident. That will help settle things down a bit."

"The charges are good, but don't be surprised if nothing changes. So far, I have been jumped in a parking lot and tailed from downtown by a couple of guys." Ricky didn't want to tell him yet that he had identified them. "Susan and my partner went to the Ronnie Jenkins rally this morning. He is a friend of Dave Finley's. We are looking at everything. She is going to fill me in when I get back to the house. We are making progress, and I have some plans for the next few days. One of my associates and myself will be at the City Council meeting on Tuesday. We got word there might be some fireworks, but who knows."

Ricky finished his beer and flagged down the bartender to pay. "How much do I owe you?"

"How does two bucks sound, sport?" Livingston responded.

"Sounds like I just bought a beer," Ricky said, and left the taproom. Back at the house, he joined the others around the fire pit to talk about the day. Susan and RJ told Ricky about the rally. Ricky thought the connection between Jenkins, Billy Thompson, and Jimmy O'Brien was something to act on.

"Let's set up gear to keep an eye on them," Ricky said.

"I brought all my surveillance gear," RJ said. "I'm thinking we set up basic trail cams looking at both houses and see what that shows us. I know we might need to go back and replace batteries if they trigger a lot. I just think they are best for this environment. Lots of hunters around here, so if they are found it may not cause any alarm."

"I agree with the trail cams, they will fit in nicely. What about listening devices?" Ricky asked.

"Yep, I have all that too. Are you thinking about bugging them?"

"I think so. I'm thinking of a two-night operation. The first night, we go and put up the trail cams. We will use that footage to develop a pattern of life and decide when we go in and bug the houses. Thoughts?" Ricky asked.

"Makes sense. I think I'm good to drive by Billy's house again. They didn't notice me. From what I remember there is a wooded area bordering the house that we can use. The key is to get a cam looking at that basement door. That's where all three headed," RJ said.

"Ok, here are the priorities of work for tomorrow. RJ, you drive by the Thompson house and develop a plan for us to put up the cams tomorrow night. I'll do the same for the O'Brien house. Susan, contact Father Tim and get him some money. Tell him it's a retainer in case something goes bad, and we need him to wear his lawyer hat. First thing in the morning, let's huddle around the monitors in the office and look at maps of the areas around the houses so we spend as little time as possible driving around them bringing unneeded attention. I think it will take a couple of hours in the morning to test all the equipment again and prep for tomorrow night. Any questions?"

RJ and Susan had no questions so the three of them sat around the fire talking until it burned out.

The next morning while drinking coffee they looked at the maps around the target houses. RJ laid out six cellular trail cams. He and Ricky tested them while Susan ensured the cellular subscription was active. She then set up one of the spare monitors to display the video feeds.

Ricky and RJ left the house at noon and went their separate ways. Ricky went back out Beaverdam Road and pulled into the YMCA parking lot which he thought backed up to the condo complex where Jimmy O'Brien lives. However, when he got there, he saw there was a big hill that he had to go up and over to get to the condo. Ricky decided to go ahead with his plan and see if it worked. He had brought a soccer ball he found in the house to play with on the field next to the tree line beside the building. After kicking the ball around for several minutes, he "accidentally" kicked it into the woods. As he went in searching for his ball, he walked through the woods up the hill, which was steeper than he expected, and then down to the edge on the condo side. After catching his breath, he looked for the best angle to the O'Brien condo. Once he found a good spot, he marked the tree to make it easier later that night. Then he picked up the ball and went back to the field.

"What are you doing?" Ricky heard as he came out of the tree line.

"I was looking for my ball, I got a bit over aggressive and kicked it in there."

"Why are you playing over here and not on the soccer field?" the girl asked.

Ricky looked to where she was pointing.

"Sorry, I didn't introduce myself. I'm Becky. I work here. We're closed on Sundays, but we don't care if people use the fields. We know families like to go out and have some fun together. I just dropped by to make sure nobody is doing anything stupid."

"Oh ok, I'm Jimi Taggert. Me and the family are renting a house nearby and I wanted to come over and see what the deal is here. So, it's no big deal if I bring the kids back later today and get some exercise? My son is a big soccer player and wants to get in a little workout. We're in town from Malibu to check out the local university," Ricky lied.

"Shouldn't be any big deal. Enjoy your stay in Asheville," Becky said as she walked down to the parking lot.

"Thanks for the info, have a good weekend," Ricky said.

Ricky kicked the ball around for a bit longer to make it look convincing, but he had the information he needed. Twenty minutes later he was back in his car. He drove around to refamiliarize himself with the area in case they needed to adjust the plan at the last minute.

At the same time Ricky was playing soccer, RJ was at the second target house. He was having a much easier time. He pulled off the road in front of the driveway and pretended to look at something on his phone. He held it up and snapped a few quick pictures. Everything matched what they had seen on the maps in the office that morning. He was done quickly and then he also drove around the area before heading back to the house.

Sunday evening, Ricky and RJ finished eating dinner and got ready for the night's fun. They were both in a good mood because the weather was in their favor. It was a cool, cloudy day. It started to drizzle with more rain forecasted for the night. They decided they would leave to place the cameras at 1:00. Target one would be the O'Brien condo and then they would go over to target two, the Thompson house. Ricky wasn't worried since this operation would be in the woods with little chance of anyone seeing or hearing them.

At 12:30, they loaded the equipment into RJ's car. His car was due to be changed out the next day anyway. They decided to bring locator devices to tag the suspects' two cars if they were home. It added a bit more risk to the night's work, but they wanted to know where these guys were from now on. Before they left, Ricky made sure Susan was monitoring the police scanner and everyone was on the group call to relay information throughout the operation. With that done, Ricky and RJ left.

RJ drove down the street and turned right, heading for Merrimon Avenue. As they turned onto Merrimon Avenue a police car pulled out of a Quik Stop gas station and pulled up behind them.

"Base, we have a police car behind us," Ricky said. Susan was still getting used to the way they worked on one of these operations, but knew she needed to adapt to them.

"Base acknowledge," she responded as she marked the time in the log. In the beginning of his private investigator career, Susan asked Ricky to write out the phrases he wanted her to use whenever he was out on something like this, which wasn't very often. She wasn't in the military, so she wasn't used to talking like he did.

As Ricky and RJ went past Beaver Lake and headed up the slight incline by the library, they changed lanes.

"Guys, he is running your plates," Susan said, and then marked it in the log. Sometimes she forgot the right words to use.

"Acknowledge."

"If he turns with us, we will divert and head towards downtown," Ricky said. RJ and Susan acknowledged, and she put a pin on the map for their current location.

"Plates check came back clear, said it was a rental. Officer Clark acknowledged," Susan said, and marked it in the log.

"We are turning toward O'Brien's condo. The police car is staying on Merrimon Avenue," Ricky advised.

As they approached the YMCA, Ricky told RJ to pull into the parking lot and directed him to spaces in a corner where they wouldn't be seen from the road. He would get out and re-trace his steps from earlier in the day through the woods, put two cameras in place, and test them with Susan before putting the tag on Jimmy's truck. Then he would return to the car, and they would move on to the Thompson house.

"Base, we are at target one and I am on foot," Ricky said. Susan and RJ acknowledged. Less than ten minutes later Ricky was at the spot he had picked out earlier in the day and placed the cameras.

"Base, the cameras are in place and I'm showing them as active," Ricky said, as he quickly walked in front of them to activate them. Ricky made a last second decision and switched the camera to always be on instead of being motion activated.

"I have good video," Susan said.

"Target truck is in the third driveway on right hand side, I'm moving to place the tag." Everyone acknowledged this and waited for his next report.

Just as Ricky was about to step out of the woods, a dog started barking. It was loud enough that RJ could hear it back at the car. Ricky froze in place, realizing the dog knew he was there. He looked to the right and saw someone walking a dog coming towards him. If he stayed where he was, the dog and dogwalker would pass within 10 feet of him and the dog would most likely be all over him.

"We are moving to plan B," Ricky said, and all acknowledged.

Ricky moved as quickly and quietly as he could, putting distance between the dog and himself. Once he was safely back at the car, he passed that information to Susan so she could log it, and RJ started the car. They pulled out of the parking lot and turned right and then an immediate right onto Beaver Ridge Lane. Coming down the left side of the road was a girl walking her dog. Staying in character, RJ gave her a big friendly wave as they passed.

"Base is there anything on the police scanner?"

"All clear," Susan said.

RJ stopped the car. Ricky got out and dropped his keys beside O'Brien's white truck. He bent down to pick them up and he placed the tag.

Back in the car and before he could even ask, Susan let them know she saw the ping of the tag on her map.

"Roger, moving to target two," Ricky said.

When they got to the bottom of the hill, they saw the girl walking the dog to their left, so they turned away from her. They wound around the Asheville Country Club golf course, keeping it on their left-hand side all the way up to a "T" intersection. Instead of turning, they went straight into the parking lot of the Country Club and switched drivers. RJ would do the camera placement at target house two. They relayed that to Susan for the log and were on their way. It was now 1:50.

Ricky drove the short distance back to Merrimon Avenue. His route scouting was paying off. Turning right, in front of Beaver Lake, they were only a few miles from target two. On the way, RJ explained where he wanted to be left off over the open phone call so Susan could track. Ricky would slow down to let RJ out, proceed past the house to the turnoff on the left and wait there for the call for a pickup. It would be very important for Susan to monitor the police scanner as well as for Ricky to look out for locals who happened to be out walking around.

There was little traffic, and the rain was still coming down. With Ricky at the wheel, RJ had not so gracefully gone from the front passenger seat to the backseat. Ricky took the right turn onto Mills Place and advised RJ and Susan they were three minutes from RJ's drop off point. Ricky drove through the two sharp turns and passed the target house on the right. Before he dropped RJ off, he told him about setting the video to on and not motion detected. About a hundred yards past the house, he stopped quickly, and RJ exited. He was into the tree line before Ricky could take off again. Ricky drove the hundred yards to the turnoff on the left, then turned so he was facing out and ready to leave. He cut the car lights.

"Drop off complete, I'm at my hold spot. Base ensure you are listening for the county sheriff at this location," Ricky said. It was now 2:15.

Susan responded but Ricky didn't understand. "Did you understand her, RJ?"

"No."

"Sorry, I was having a snack. I know what I'm listening for," Susan snapped. She was both hungry and tired. There had been a lot going on the last few days and he understood, everyone was worn out.

RJ stood quietly in the woods for several minutes listening for any movement or sounds. He then took one last look and ran across the street into another small, wooded area that he could follow around to the back of the house. Five minutes later he was in place looking at the back of the target house, specifically at the door to the basement where he saw Thompson, O'Brien, and Jenkins go earlier. He placed three cameras about ten yards apart to get the best coverage.

"Three cameras are placed and active. White Bronco is here. I'm moving to tag the vehicle," RJ said.

"I have good video from the cameras," Susan replied as she saw RJ start out of the tree line towards the Bronco.

"You're clear," Ricky said.

As RJ reached the Bronco, a motion detection light came on. He dropped to the ground beside the rear wheel. The front door of the house opened, and Billy Thompson walked out.

"The guy that came out of the house is standing to your left looking around. Stay where you are," Susan passed to everyone. She was the eyes of the operation now. "He is moving towards you, still on your left side."

"I have headlights coming down the road towards the house," Ricky advised. "It's slowing down and looks like it's pulling in."

RJ saw the headlights turn into the driveway and come toward where he was hiding and where Billy was standing.

"It's a pickup truck, but I can't tell the color," Susan said.

The new arrival pulled up next to the Bronco and stopped. RJ rolled under the Bronco just in time. He saw the interior light of the truck come on as the door opened. Then he saw a woman's knee-high boots and tight jeans step out and give Billy a hug. They were less than five feet from where RJ was laying. RJ heard Billy call her Sara, so it had to be Sara Dunn. RJ moved further away from them, so he was closer to the passenger side of the Bronco and close to the bushes lining the house.

"Billy is moving around looking for something," Susan advised.

He was as still as he could be, but ready to move if he needed to. Ricky had his hands on the ignition in case he had to get RJ out of there fast.

"Billy is walking back to the house," Susan said.

RJ heard the door of the house close and Billy's footsteps coming back toward the Bronco. Then the driver's door opened, and Billy got in. Sara walked around to the passenger side. At the same time, RJ rolled back over toward the driver's side waiting for the Bronco to pull away. As the Bronco pulled away and the rear wheels cleared RJ, he quickly rolled under the pickup truck, which he now saw was a blue chevy, and did not move again.

"I'm under the truck and placing a spare tag I brought," RJ told the team.

"I see the new tag," Susan replied.

"The Bronco is leaving and turning left out of the driveway. Hold another few minutes, RJ," Ricky directed. "Susan, while I'm picking up RJ, watch the Bronco to see where it goes. Thompson and Dunn are in it."

"You are clear, RJ. I'm moving to the pickup point," Ricky said and all acknowledged.

Back in the car, RJ described everything that happened as they drove back to the house.

By the time they got to the office, the Bronco had stopped briefly at a house in Weaverville and was driving back towards Mills Place.

"Sara Dunn's house," Susan told the guys. "My guess is Thompson drove her back to her house after she dropped off the blue Chevy."

They had a quick review of the early morning's activities, and it was off to bed.

By mid-day Monday, they were all up and drinking coffee while reviewing the video from both locations. The car tags indicated everyone was at work for the day.

Chapter 8

It was still raining when Jimmy walked into City Hall. He took the elevator to the second floor and found his way to the council chamber. Jimmy walked to the front of the room where a seat had been saved for him and looked around before sitting down. The room was set up the usual way, a semi-circle dais with name plates for each council member with the Mayor in the center to control the meeting and room. Jimmy knew the two Councilmembers running for reelection were the last two on the right. Carnes or Bradley, which one didn't matter, whoever replied to him would be his target, but he was hoping for crooked Bradley. He liked the fact that the room was full, with people standing in the back along the walls. The Council members looked surprised as they entered the chamber. It was rare to see this many people attending.

Ricky and RJ drove separately, parked on opposite sides of town, and walked to City Hall. It was a coincidence that they arrived at the door at the same time. Not acknowledging each other, one held the door for the other and they entered the council chamber. Ricky sat just inside the door in the last row and RJ went to the left and stood in the far corner. Ricky saw Jimmy O'Brien enter and go straight to the front of the room a few minutes before the Mayor called the meeting to order.

The Mayor went through all the required procedures, which Jimmy thought was silly. 'Just get on with it,' he thought. He couldn't help but stare at Bradley who was wearing a bright yellow flower shirt like he's on some island somewhere. Jimmy moved to the edge of his seat as the Mayor announced the next agenda item would be the new park and pickle ball courts. Almost everyone in attendance booed and raised homemade signs against the new park. They all knew it was nothing more than a tax increase. The Mayor banged her gavel to regain control of her meeting. She passed the floor over to Councilwoman Bobbi Carnes to read the proposal. Jimmy felt the Mayor was giving Carnes facetime with the media and audience by having her read the proposal. After she finished reading, she invited comments from the floor.

Jimmy was on his feet before Councilwoman Carnes was done.

"This is crazy," he said. "What are you doing? Building a park when we have other issues more important." This drew a few cheers from the crowd and the signs went up again. "This town is out of control. Councilwoman, I know you haven't lived here long, but you need to drive around and open your eyes. You narrowed the roads, yet we have an increase in traffic. You expanded the airport, but getting to it takes twice as long. The interstate has been under construction for years with no end in sight. Tourists walk around with no regard for cars. We locals try to go to and from work but all we do is dodge people downtown." Jimmy was starting to roll now. He could feel it and so could the crowd.

"Sir, everything you noted is progress for our town. I don't understand your point," Councilwoman Carnes replied while Jimmy took a breath.

"No, it's not progress. My point is taking care of the homeless, enhancing the infrastructure BEFORE growth, and getting the tourism under control would be progress and a better use of time and money," Jimmy said as the room erupted into loud cheers and applause. The Mayor banged her gavel again, harder this time.

"I think we've heard enough," the Councilwoman said. "Mayor, I think we should take a vote."

"No, you haven't heard enough. You seem to have forgotten one very important thing," Jimmy said, staring at her.

"And what is that?" she asked, returning his stare.

He had her now, she was talking to him directly. She had lost her composure.

"All of you have clearly forgotten that you work for us. We elected you to represent us, the people of Asheville. You are failing terribly. Maybe this is how it's done in other parts of the country but it's not how it works here. I used to think politics was better on the local level and the problem is with the state government and up in D.C." People were getting on their feet now. Not only could they feel the passion, but they agreed. "I was wrong, you're all the same. Again, you work for us, and you don't get it. We don't care about pickleball and parks right now. There's plenty of that stuff already. We want our city back!" Jimmy yelled as the room erupted. "Buckle up buttercup, we're coming for your seat!" Jimmy yelled. As Jimmy walked out of the room, everyone in attendance turned their signs around to show the other side: 'Save Asheville Elect Ronnie Jenkins City Council.'

Sitting in the back of the room, Ricky glanced at RJ as Jimmy's speech started to unfold. Ricky had kept his phone out since he had a group text with Susan and RJ. Susan said the meeting was being streamed online, so she was watching and recording it at the house. The first time the crowd raised their signs, Ricky and RJ could see the backsides, so they knew what was coming. Ricky decided to slip out the back as Jimmy was working everyone into a frenzy. He saw his old high school classmate Nick Zika was there, and felt bad he didn't get to say hello, but Ricky was working.

Ricky walked out of the building and saw a crowd gathering at the amphitheater in front of City Hall where he sat just a few days before. He walked over to see what was going on. Ronnie Jenkins was on the stage capitalizing on the meeting and trying to keep the momentum as people came out. Ricky thought it was smart of him to have set up a two-pronged attack. Jimmy got them stirred up inside, and Ronnie grabbed them again outside. He was using the same messaging that Jimmy had started inside, and it was working. Ronnie ended with the phrase that would soon take over Asheville: buckle up buttercup, we're coming.

It was almost 9:00 when they all got back to the house. Susan had the local paper online edition up waiting for them. The headline was "Buckle Up Buttercup" with pictures of Jimmy O'Brien and Ronnie Jenkins. They went outside to the firepit to have drinks and talk through the night. Ricky decided they needed to hear what Billy, Jimmy, and Ronnie were up to, and the only way to do that was to plant listening devices in their houses. Over drinks, Ricky and RJ developed a plan for the next night, Wednesday. Ricky would do the entry at the Thompson house and RJ would do the O'Brien house. A couple of hours later, they had the outline of the operation for the following night and went back inside to turn on the news.

"I checked on the cars before we came out here, they're all together at the Thompson house," Susan reported.

"Hello Asheville, thanks for tuning into WAVL. I'm Darby Jones. Buckle up buttercup, the Asheville City Council meeting erupted into chaos when a local business owner made an impassioned speech about his view of our city. The Mayor lost control quickly and failed to get it back until after he finished. Jimmy O'Brien owns Cats Landscaping with Dave Finley, who was killed a couple of weeks ago by a drunk driver. He gave an unexpected speech imploring the Council to fix the city and to cut back on tourism and pickle ball. He finished by addressing Councilwoman Carnes directly, telling her to 'buckle up buttercup' because they were coming for her seat. The full house erupted in cheers as they held up signs that said, 'Save Asheville Elect Ronnie Jenkins City Council.' When the Mayor finally regained control, the Council voted in favor of placing the new pickle ball court and park on the November ballot, raising property taxes. After the meeting, Ronnie Jenkins held a rally outside City Hall with hundreds of people cheering him on. We also caught up with the other local candidate, Nick Zika. He agreed the new park and pickle ball courts should wait until the infrastructure in Asheville is addressed. This election has taken a turn, and we will keep an eye on it for you."

Billy turned off WAVL when the report about the meeting and the rally was over. He went to the fridge and got celebratory beers for Ronnie and Jimmy. "That was a good show you two put on. Darby's looking good tonight, don't you think Jimmy?" Billy said with a wink.

"I had a hard time holding my tongue about that crooked councilman. You leave Darby alone, I have my eye on her," Jimmy said laughing.

You did a great job getting them spun up for me," Ronnie said. "After thinking through everything and especially about the crooked politician and brewery owner, I agree about the warehouse. Let's go over the plan one more time and do it."

"We assumed we would move forward with it, so you probably saw Sara's truck outside. It's gassed up and ready to go. We both know the address of where we are going but I wrote it down as well," Billy said. "I talked to Bobby. Even though it's his day off, he will be in the area tomorrow night."

"I have the gas cans filled up. I did a couple at a time and at different gas stations to not draw attention. Paid by cash too. We are planning on leaving here around one in the morning and it will probably take ten minutes to get there. The biggest problem will be the door. I'm sure the door will be locked, but it's on the backside facing the river, which will buy us some time. Once inside, dump the gas, light it, and get out of there. I drove by it on the way here tonight after the meeting. That was about 9:30 and there were no cars in the parking lot then," Jimmy said.

"I drove by the other night before Sara dropped off the truck. That was about 11:30 and it was empty then, too. I think we are good on that but if we show up and there is any sign of someone, we are out of there." Billy said.

"Sounds like a solid plan. When you are done, park Sara's truck in her garage and tell her to leave it there. She'll figure it out but don't tell her anything. What about the distraction?" Ronnie asked.

"It's all taken care of," Billy said. "It will be about 10:30 before they close. It should cause some chaos which will draw attention to the middle of downtown."

"Just so you guys know, tomorrow I will be all over town. Now that my name is out there, I'm kicking the campaign into high gear. Don't call or text about the warehouse, I'll be watching the news and will know."

When they were done covering the plan and had one more beer to toast the good night they had, it was time for them all to head for home.

Chapter 9

"Good evening, we have breaking news out of downtown Asheville. About twenty minutes ago, three downtown businesses were attacked. The individuals threw sledgehammers at the windows of some breweries. We are working on gathering more information, but the businesses are believed to be the Asheville Beer Facility, Coxe Ave Brewery, and Circus Act Brewery. There is a heavy police presence, and ambulances have been called to the scene indicating multiple injuries. We will continue to follow this story and will provide updates at the 11 o'clock news. I'm Darby Jones. We will send you back to normal broadcasting."

"You guys better get in here and see this," Susan yelled. "An attack downtown against our clients. I have the report pulled up online for you."

Ricky and RJ ran to the office to see the news. It wasn't good. They knew it made planting the listening devices even more important.

"You are going to have to keep a good eye on everything tonight," Ricky said to Susan. "The police scanners and the news will be key. Let us know if you think anything else big happens."

At 11:00 Ricky and RJ started getting ready. They decided to wear their flight suits from their days at The Command. It took some doing and several minutes but they both managed to cram themselves into their flight suits. It had obviously been a while since they wore them.

"You look like a fucking moron," RJ said.

"As if you look like Tom Cruise in Top Gun," Ricky responded.

It was one of those conversations that veterans could have with one another. There is a special bond because they understand each other. It's even deeper for people who deployed together. RJ and Ricky were in that club.

"Thompson and O'Brien just loaded what looked like gas cans into Sara Dunn's truck," Susan said as she walked into the room, looking at them oddly. All three went to the office and huddled around the screens and watched as the truck drove off.

"Two things just happened. The first is our job tonight just got easier because they are gone, and we have the truck tagged. Second, something else is up, and it doesn't look good. I don't think it's a coincidence there was an attack downtown and now they are leaving the way they are. Susan, we need you to be on top of your game for the next few hours. Keep a close eye on that truck and a close ear on us and the police scanner," Ricky ordered. "RJ let's go and get this done. One more time to make sure we are all on the same page, the Thompson house is first, and I'm doing the entry. Then we move to the O'Brien house and RJ does the entry. Susan, keep your regular cell phone handy with Father Tim's number ready in the event everything goes to shit. Let's go."

Ricky and RJ loaded the car and headed for the first target house. It was a familiar route now, so they were at ease. RJ put Evanescence on the radio and turned it up. Other than the music, they drove in silence. As they went up the hill at the beginning of Mills Place and through the two sharp curves leading to Billy Thompson's house, Susan gave them an update.

"Thompson and O'Brien stopped at what looks like a warehouse down on Riverside Drive which runs along the French Broad River. WAVL is reporting at least six people hurt in the sledgehammer attack."

"Copy," Ricky responded. "We are at the parking spot and getting ready to be on foot."

Ricky had found a spot in the woods where they could park the car without it being seen from the road. Ricky and RJ would be on foot with RJ positioning himself so he could see both the back of the Thompson house and the road. After parking the car, Ricky and RJ got out and sat quietly in the woods for several minutes to make sure nobody had seen them. Feeling sure they were alone, they stood and headed for their next checkpoint. They crossed the road at the same place where RJ had crossed a couple of days earlier and got back to the tree line as fast as possible. They sat for several more minutes and listened. Hearing nothing, Ricky moved to the closest point to the back door. RJ went another hundred yards to the spot he had picked to keep watch. Once in position they again sat for about five minutes to listen and watch.

"Anything new on the guys by the river?" Ricky whispered into the phone.

"No," Susan replied.

"We are in position and I'm about to move to the door. RJ, I'll move in one minute."

"Copy," was RJ's reply.

Ricky broke out of the cover of the woods and quickly moved to the basement door. He already had his lock pick set out, so he didn't have to waste a lot of time. As he got to the door, the neighbor's dog started barking. He couldn't be distracted by the dog. Ricky kept telling himself, 'Don't worry about the dog just worry about the lock.' As luck would have it, the door was unlocked. He entered the basement and again he was lucky as there was a Busch Light neon sign on which gave enough light for him to see.

Ricky did a quick scan of the room. Bar on the right with bar stools and two chairs with a table between them on the other side of the room. A TV on the far side, opposite the door he had come in. He decided to plant the first bug under the bar overhang by the bar stools, then one on the table between the two chairs, and a third behind a lamp on top of the beer fridge.

"You have been inside one minute," RJ said.

"Copy, one minute," Ricky said as he got to work. "First bug is planted, under an overhang of the bar. Do you see it?" he whispered.

"I show it as active," Susan replied.

"You have been inside two minutes."

Ricky slipped behind the bar to the beer fridge and placed the second bug behind the lamp. "Second bug placed. Do you see it?"

"I see two active bugs."

Finally, Ricky moved across the room to the table between the two chairs and placed the third bug. "Third bug is placed under a table between two chairs. Do you see it?"

"I show three bugs as active."

"You have been inside for five minutes. Time to leave," RJ said.

"Roger, I am at the door ready to leave. Am I clear?" Ricky whispered.

"Hold on, there is car coming down the road." A few seconds later, "You are clear to the tree line," RJ advised.

Ricky opened the basement door, took one last look at the room so he could sketch it out later, ensured the door was still unlocked, and closed it. A few seconds later he was safely back in the woods.

"I'm in the woods no issues," Ricky whispered.

"I'm moving to you," RJ replied.

Once they were back together, they told Susan they were heading to the car and would let her know when they got there.

"Guys, something is going on. I think something with our two friends. I recommend not going to the second house and getting back here," Susan said.

Ricky and RJ gave each other a concerned look because she had never gotten involved operationally before. They moved carefully and retraced their steps through the woods to the road. Again, they waited several minutes, and all was quiet. It was a very long few minutes because they were anxious about what was going on. The time passed without issues and Ricky and RJ moved across the street to the car. After getting in and storing their equipment, they let Susan know they were heading for the house.

Billy walked up to the door of the warehouse and tried the door. As expected, it was locked. Several minutes later he was getting nowhere with opening it. Jimmy had parked the truck close enough to the door to be able to talk to Billy and move the gas cans in as soon as he got the door open. Finally, Billy had enough. He stood up to kick the door. On the third kick, the door popped open.

Billy reached into the bed of the truck and took two of the four cans, setting two on the ground and taking the other two with him into the warehouse. It smelled like beer. There was pallet after pallet of hops, yeast, and grains. The inside was much smaller than he expected. Things were neatly sorted with small signs indicating which brewery owned which section. He moved to the center of the warehouse and started dumping gas everywhere. When he finished with the first two cans, he went back for the others. Billy grabbed the last two cans and asked Jimmy if he had seen anything.

"No, but you're being louder than shit. If anyone is walking on the trail beside the river, we are done. How's it going inside?"

"That damn door sucked. I just dumped the first two cans in the middle. I'll work my way out from there with these two and then light it. Should be just a few more minutes," Billy told him.

Billy disappeared back into the warehouse. He tried to speed it up because he knew the longer they were there, the more likely they were to get caught. As he emptied the last of the cans, he brought them back to truck. No need to leave anything behind. Then he went back into the warehouse.

Jimmy could smell the smoke before he saw Billy. It smelled more like beer was brewing than a fire, but then he saw the flames. Billy ran out of the warehouse and jumped into the truck as the fire grew. Jimmy slowly pulled out of the parking lot and turned towards downtown. He had decided not to go home the same way they had come. As Jimmy drove away, he looked in the rearview mirror and saw the flames engulfing the warehouse. He could hear sirens heading towards them. As he turned onto Merrimon Avenue, he saw the flashing lights of fire trucks behind him. There were a couple of other cars on the road, which made him feel better. The fire trucks might remember one truck on the road, but there were at least four or five other cars near Jimmy and Billy.

Driving the speed limit the entire way, Jimmy pulled into Billy's driveway 15 minutes later and let Billy out. Billy jumped into his Bronco and followed Jimmy to Sara's house to park the truck and bring him back. By the time they got back to Billy's it was 2:30. As they pulled into the driveway, Billy got a text from Bobby that they were clear, no witnesses.

Ricky and RJ got back to the house at about 2:00 and went straight to the office where Susan was waiting for them.

"What's going on?" Ricky asked as he popped a Miller High Life.

"The police scanner started going crazy. A warehouse caught on fire down near the French Broad River. When I plotted the address, it is where our two friends were. It gets worse. The warehouse is owned by our clients," Susan told them.

Ricky thought for a moment, taking a swallow of beer. "OK, did you record the car tracking and the cams from when they left the Thompson house?" Ricky asked.

"Yea, you know I record everything," Susan said.

"Good, make copies and save them..." Ricky said.

"...to the external hard drive and to a thumb drive, already done," Susan said.

"Where are they now?" RJ asked.

"They brought the truck they used back to Sara Dunn's house. If our tags are working, they are now pulling up to Billy Thompson's house. I'll bring up the bugs to see if they are in the basement," Susan said, turning back to her computers.

Within seconds they heard the voices of Thompson and O'Brien. Susan ensured it was recording but knew it could never be used officially, since they were placed illegally. The three of them listened as Billy Thompson and Jimmy O'Brien relived the entire night from start to finish. It was obvious they were still on an adrenaline high. Their voices gave that away.

"Did you guys pick up on Thompson saying something about a crooked politician and business owner, and how they are to blame for them doing this tonight?" Ricky said.

"It sounded like he said something about vote buying but I couldn't tell," RJ added.

"That's new. What do they know that we don't? One more thing to add to the board," Ricky said.

When the voices stopped at the other end, it was 3:30. Ricky sent Father Tim a text to set up a lunch meeting at Mitchell's Sports Bar and they all went to bed. Ricky had a feeling it was going to be a long and interesting day.

The next morning, Ronnie got in his 4Runner hoping for a short drive to work when his phone rang. He was a little surprised to see it was Sara.

"Hey Sara, is everything ok?" Ronnie asked.

"We need to talk. Can you meet me at the coffee shop in Weaverville?" Sara said.

"Sure. I'm on my way to work but can be there in about 15 minutes," he said.

Sara found a parking place and then a table inside and sat down to wait for Ronnie to show up. He was right on schedule. About 15 minutes after their phone call, he walked in and waved to her.

"Do you want a cup of coffee or anything?" Ronnie asked.

'Yes please," she responded.

After taking a sip of her coffee Sara said to Ronnie, "What the hell is going on with you guys? Billy called a few days ago and asked to borrow my truck. Naturally I said yes. Then he returned it early this morning, it must have been around 2 or 3. I woke up and saw that a brewery warehouse was burned down. So, I'm asking you, what the hell have you guys done?"

"Sara, you know how we all feel about what Asheville has turned into. That includes Dave. None of us like it," he said.

"Disliking all the tourists is one thing but burning down a warehouse, using my truck, is another. You guys better know what you're doing. It makes more sense why Dave was always calling Bobby. Is he involved in this, too?" Sara asked. She was finding it hard to not yell and attract attention.

"Sitting back and doing nothing is how we got to this point. You know that."

"I already lost my fiancé. You guys are some of the best friends I have. I don't want to lose you guys, too. Plus, it's just wrong. There are other ways to effect change. You're running for city council. If you win that gives you an avenue to do something about it," she said.

"Remember Dave's parents? They were forced out by the taxes and moved in with you guys. That wasn't right. Then Dave was killed by a drunk driving tourist. Enough is enough. Think about how many people we know that used to live here and had to move somewhere else in the county because they couldn't afford it anymore. Plus, you don't know the whole story," Ronnie replied.

"Listen to yourself. This isn't the Ronnie Jenkins I know. All you guys need to really think about what you're doing," Sara said.

"I have this under control," he said.

Sara got up and left while Ronnie sat and thought about the conversation. After a few minutes he got up to leave, but one thing Sara said was sticking in his head: 'it's wrong.' On his way to work, Ronnie told the others about his conversation with Sara.

Chapter 10

Ricky and Susan walked into Mitchell's Sports Bar at 12:30.

"Ricky T!" Kenny yelled from behind the bar.

"You're the man, Kenny!" Ricky yelled back.

He saw Father Tim was waiting for them at their corner table. Ricky took his seat across the table from him, and Susan was in her seat looking at the menu. When the waitress came over, everyone but Ricky ordered lunch. Susan knew he was in his work zone and if she let him, he would go days without eating. She ordered for him, and they got down to business.

"Did you see the news this morning about the warehouse?" Ricky asked Father Tim.

"I did, but I'm not hearing anything about it yet," he responded.

"I know Susan gave you a retainer. Does that cover client confidentiality for the three of us with you?"

"Yeah, and you know you guys would have it anyway. What's going on?" Father Tim asked as the waitress brought their food and another round of drinks.

As they ate, Ricky told the story of the day before. Not leaving out anything, he told Father Tim about his and RJ's operation and what they had recorded from O'Brien and Thompson.

"So, Jimmy O'Brien went from his big speech to the City Council to setting a warehouse on fire?" Father Tim summarized. "Doesn't seem very smart. He is famous all over town. Everywhere I go, someone is talking about him. Ronnie Jenkins is suddenly all over town. Yesterday morning, he showed up at our local minister's breakfast. He sat with us for a while and discussed what he thought was wrong with the city. Nothing crazy, pretty much a combination of their speeches from Tuesday. I heard that later that morning he attended a Woman's Business Leaders luncheon and did the same.

He is jumping on the momentum. I don't know if it will be enough." Father Tim took another bite while Ricky let all that information soak in.

Before Ricky could say anything, his phone rang. It was Clif Jordan.

"Hi Clif," Ricky said, taking a sip of beer.

"We need to talk. Did you see what happened last night?" Clif said in an annoyed voice.

"I did, and I am coming to see you this afternoon if that works. I'm finishing lunch with Father Tim and will head your way when we're done," Ricky said hoping to calm him down.

"That will work. I'll be at the brewery all afternoon. Look, Ricky, we are starting to lose money and last night hurt. I hope you have something for us." Click.

Ricky set his phone down and went back to his lunch. He almost got a bite of his sandwich when his phone rang again. This time it was his personal phone and not his burner. He didn't recognize the number.

"Ricky Temple."

"Mr. PI, this is Lt. Dalton from the Asheville Police. We met last week after you got beat up."

"It's still private investigator and yes, I remember you well. What can I do for you?"

"I was hoping you could come down to the station and talk with us. See if you know anything about everything going on around town."

"I'm sure meeting with you will be as enjoyable as going to the dentist. I'm eating lunch right now but can be there in about an hour," Ricky offered.

"An hour works, I believe you know the way," Lt. Dalton said. Click.

Susan and Father Tim stared at Ricky, but he didn't say anything when he got off the phone. He was determined to get a bite of sandwich and some beer in him.

"That was Lt. Dalton from the police department. He wants to meet and discuss the events going on around town," Ricky said while using air quotes when he said events around town. "It might be a good idea for you to come with me, Tim. How's your afternoon look?"

"It's Thursday, my day off. So, I'm good. Meant to ask, where is RJ, anyway?"

"After what we heard the other night about the crooked politician, I asked him to investigate something. He is also due to change cars and had to go all the way out to the airport this time – and you know how bad traffic is going that way." Ricky turned toward Susan. "I'll bring Susan home when we are done here and then meet you downtown. I told Dalton I'd be there in an hour, so I'll show in an hour and half. Susan, fill RJ in on all of this. Until I get back, keep an eye on the cars and listen to that basement."

It was closer to 2:30 when Ricky met Father Tim outside the police station. He had sent a text to Clif Jordan while driving to the police station to let him know he was delayed. Clif didn't like it but understood.

"Why is he here?" Lt. Dalton snapped as Ricky and Father Tim walked in.

"He's my lawyer," Ricky shot back.

"He's a priest."

"I told you this guy was sharp, doesn't miss a thing," Ricky said to Father Tim. "He's also a lawyer, passed the bar and everything. Can we get on with it?"

"Let's start with why you showed up with a lawyer?" Dalton said.

"Mr. Temple is a longtime client. He told me about your encounter, to put it nicely, last week so I advised him to ensure I was with him if he ever had to talk to you again," said Father Tim. "What do you want with my client?"

"I'll put it this way. Your client, as you like to say, showed up in town and suddenly things started happening," Dalton said as Officer Clark walked up behind him. "He was found by Officer Clark here beaten up in a parking lot after meeting with some brewery owners, then we have a chaotic City Council meeting which your client attended, now we have a warehouse fire that is owned by three of the breweries downtown. The three breweries your client met with own the warehouse."

"Lieutenant don't forget a car chase into the Stein Mart parking lot in North Asheville," Officer Clark added.

Ricky perked up immediately. He knew he had never told the police who he was working for or why he was even in town. With Clark adding the part about the chase, which had no police involvement, he was beginning to get one of his uneasy feelings.

"Sorry, is there a question in there I missed?" Father Tim asked.

"Lieutenant, would it be possible for me to confer with my counsel in private for a few minutes?" Ricky asked, already standing, and not giving Lt. Dalton a chance to respond.

"For you, anything. Use the interview room around the corner on the left."

"Did you catch all that?" Ricky asked Father Tim as they closed the door to the interview room. "He brought up things he shouldn't know. There's a leak and now I think I know who it is."

Before Father Tim could answer, Ricky took out his phone and called Susan and put her on speakerphone. Susan said RJ was with her but was about to leave on the other matter. She asked how it was going at the police station.

Ricky ignored her question and got to the point because he didn't know how much time they had, "We are still here. I need you to look up Officer Clark and see if you can find anything out about him."

"Not much about him. Born and raised in Asheville and has been on the police force a little over six years," Susan said. "I was just about to dig into Sara Dunn as well. Are you ready for this? She was married once before, and Dunn is her married name. She got a divorce 10 years ago and never went back to her maiden name, Clark. Stay with me, I'm still looking. Here it is. She has a brother, Bobby Clark who happens to be Officer Bobby Clark of the Asheville Police Department."

"Bingo. Gotta run. We'll talk later," Ricky said.

Ricky filled Father Tim in on everything as quickly as he could. Jimmy O'Brien, Ronnie Jenkins, and Billy Thompson had a connection within the police department via the late Dave Finley's fiancée. Sara probably knew some of what was going on and used her younger brother to help keep her fiancé out of trouble. Ricky also told Father Tim there were no police involved in that car chase, but he had seen a police car roll through the parking lot after he and RJ had left. Ricky's guess was Billy or Jimmy called their police pal, Bobby Clark, for backup. That would explain how he knew about the incident.

"Look, I don't how deep in the police department this goes. I hope it stops with Bobby Clark and Dalton isn't involved, but who knows. We need to get out of here until we can figure things out," Ricky said.

"Ok, I'll get us out of here." Father Tim opened the door and led Ricky back to the squad room where Lt. Dalton and Officer Clark were waiting. Father Tim said, "What are you charging my client with?"

"Nothing yet. We just wanted to know what he knows," Lt. Dalton said.

"If you aren't pressing charges, we are leaving." Ricky and Father Tim walked out.

"What is this car chase you were talking about?" Dalton asked the more junior officer after they left.

"I was on patrol in the area and received a phone call from a concerned citizen and went over to investigate. I saw a car that looked like Temple's."

Outside, Ricky asked Father Tim to go back to the house and fill in Susan and RJ on everything. He still had to get to the brewery to talk things over with Clif Jordan.

RJ waited outside City Hall for Phil Bradley to come out. He wasn't hard to miss because he was wearing a bright orange tropical shirt with birds all over it. RJ followed people many times throughout his career and is skilled at keeping his distance without being seen or losing his target. Bradley walked toward a parking garage across the street. Knowing the correct walking pace, RJ ensured he arrived at the crosswalk while the signal was still on and crossed with Bradley.

RJ got to his car before Bradley and waited for the councilman to exit. When he did, RJ pulled in behind him and the two cars drove to the bypass that goes through downtown Asheville. They started south towards Hendersonville and fifty minutes later, RJ watched as Bradley pulled into a bank parking lot. Bradley parked and walked across the lot into The Tavern. RJ found a spot and followed.

Once inside RJ remembered nobody knew him so he got a table as close to where Bradley was sitting as he could. Then he waited. Feeling it was odd he drove all the way to Hendersonville just for lunch, he pulled his phone out ready to get pictures if his gut feeling was right. It was. Just five minutes later, another guy walked in and joined Bradley at the table.

RJ didn't know if it was just two friends having lunch or if it was connected to everything going on in Asheville. It wasn't busy and the staff hadn't turned the music on yet. RJ turned on the audio recording on his phone and set it as close to the Bradley table as he could.

"Did you think about what we discussed?" the newcomer asked Bradley.

"Like I said the last time we met, we are good to go. You just better get the votes you say you can get," Bradley said. Phil Bradley then reached into his coat pocket and took out an envelope that obviously had cash in it and slid it across the table to his lunch partner.

When RJ heard the key words 'in business' and 'votes' he reached over to get his phone and stopped the recording. He opened his camera and acted like any other tourist and started taking selfies. He got clear pictures of the envelope being passed.

When the two left, RJ looked over everything he had before calling Ricky. Listening to the audio it was clear the two lunch mates were discussing vote buying.

"What's up, RJ?" Ricky said, answering the phone.

"I followed Bradley from City Hall. We ended up at a tavern in Hendersonville. He met someone and I was able to get a little audio, that I will try to clean up. Then an envelope was passed. I got good pics of the pass," RJ said.

"Wow. Ok. Who was the other guy?"

"Not sure. I haven't seen him before, but I will send you what I got. Hold on," RJ said.

"Oh no. I know who it is," Ricky said. "It's one of our clients. It's Brian Johnson, the owner of Coxe Ave Brewery. Send the pics to

Susan and ask her to print them out, make a couple of copies. I'm about to go into a meeting with the owners now. I'll see you back at the house," Ricky said. Click.

To clear his head, Ricky walked to the brewery for his meeting. It gave him a chance to get some fresh air and decide his next step. Ricky entered Circus Act Brewery and saw Clif Jordan and Mike Lamb. There was a Miller High Life on the bar.

"What's going on? We need an update," Mike said.

"Gentlemen let's sit down somewhere private," Ricky said as he took off his Red Sox hat.

Clif led the three of them to his office.

"On the phone you said you were losing money, but in our first meeting you said the boycott was having little effect," Ricky said as they all sat down.

Mike and Clif looked at each other and nodded. "In our first meeting, we still weren't sure about you, so we held back. The fact is the boycott is having some effect. Not a lot but enough for us to notice. Like I told you before, we are losing the local business, which we need during the winter months. The fire last night will hurt a lot. That will put us behind on brewing beer and stocking up as the holidays approach," Clif said. "Brian isn't here now because, as you may know, there are about 50 breweries in the area which is how we got the nickname of Beer City. He is trying to line up help and borrow supplies from them so we can keep going. As soon as we are done here, Clif and I will be out doing the same. Now what do you have for us?"

"I was wondering why Brian wasn't here," Ricky said. He filled the two of them in on his investigation but decided to leave the part out about Brian until he knew more. He started with him getting beat up after their first meeting and his first meeting with Lt. Dalton and Officer Clark. He continued with the car chase and his backup that came into town to help him out.

"We decided to put up cameras at the houses of the people we suspect are behind all this. I won't bore you with details, but after the City Council meeting, we decided to listen in on those houses as well. It just so happened that while we were at their houses, they were setting your warehouse on fire."

"Who are they, exactly?" Clif asked.

"Jimmy O'Brien, Billy Thompson, and most likely Ronnie Jenkins," Ricky answered. "You can include Dave Finley before he died."

"We need to get this to the police, then," Mike demanded.

Ricky then walked them through the meeting he had just had at the police department and his revelation about Officer Bobby Clark. He explained that he didn't know how deep in the police department their help went, so he was steering clear of the police for now. Ricky then stressed that all the information he just gave them remained between them but of course they should tell Brian. Ricky stressed they needed to keep their mouths shut so he could work. They all agreed, and Ricky left annoyed. It wasn't the first time a client had held information back from him, and he didn't like it.

It had been a long day and Ricky was looking forward to getting back to the house and doing nothing for the rest of the day.

At 11:10 Ricky jumped up in bed, unable to breathe. This was his second episode in as many weeks. He needed to see light. It was too dark. After calming his heart rate and catching his breath a bit, he went to the living room to open the curtains and see outside. He didn't want to wake Susan as he knew she needed her sleep.

Ricky turned around from opening the curtains to see RJ standing there.

"It happened again, didn't it?"

"Yeah," Ricky said. "Same old thing. I wonder if the stress of everything going on here is triggering something."

"What does Susan think?"

"Not too surprising, she wants me to see a doctor. But I hate them. Nothing ever seems to get fixed, and I just end up with bills," Ricky said.

"I talk to a lot of the guys from The Command. Several of them have the same issue and they went to see someone to talk things through with. It seems to have helped them," RJ said. "Promise me you'll go see someone when this is all over. Don't do it for me and Susan, do it for yourself. Get some peace of mind, brother."

"Ok, when this is over." With that, RJ went back to bed, leaving Ricky to sit in a chair staring out the window at the streetlight.

Chapter 11

"Coming up on the evening news, we have new information about the warehouse fire on Riverside Drive earlier this morning. Officials tell us it was intentionally set but they have no suspects at this time. Also, the City Council will be releasing a tourism economic impact report tomorrow afternoon. We also have learned the six people injured in the sledgehammer throwing assault have been treated and released from the hospital. Some positive news this evening, Asheville was selected over Smithfield and New Bern to host the Adult Co-ed Softball final four and championship. The agreement is for five years and will start next year. Lastly, we have a cute story about a family of bears that wandered through downtown last night. I'm Darby Jones and I look forward to seeing you this evening."

The house on Graystone Road was close enough to Jimmy's to make it his first stop of the day. As he pulled up to the house, it looked like nobody was home. He was disappointed because he wanted to talk to the hot renter again.

Jimmy got out of his truck and unloaded his equipment. He had five houses on the schedule for the day, so he needed to get going if he wanted to finish before dark.

"Is it Friday already?" Susan asked as she walked over to Jimmy's truck.

"Oh, good morning, ma'am. It is Friday. I didn't think anyone was home."

"The sun comes in the front window, so I keep the curtains closed, especially when I'm watching TV. Do you want a cup of coffee or water before you start? It's a bit chilly this morning," Susan offered.

"Well, sure that would be great. I only got one cup this morning," Jimmy lied as they both turned and walked toward the front door. He really didn't have time for this, but he also didn't want to pass up time talking to her. It's rare that a customer even speaks to him unless they have a complaint.

As they walked in the front door, Susan pointed Jimmy to a seat in the living room. He sat down as she went to the kitchen and poured a cup of coffee.

"Do you want cream or sugar?" she yelled from the kitchen.

"No, black is fine."

"I saw on the news a lot of crazy stuff going on in town. What's it all about? Wait, aren't you the guy from the City Council meeting a few nights ago?" she asked while handing him his coffee.

"Oh, you saw that. Yeah, that was me."

"What's going on around here? I saw the news this morning about some warehouse fire that was set on purpose, an attack downtown or something, and you were giving the City Council a piece of your mind. What gives?" she asked.

"I don't know anything about the warehouse fire except what I saw on WAVL before I came over here. I did hear it was owned by a few of the breweries downtown and I know some people don't like them and the tourists they bring in. See, Asheville used to be a quiet mountain town. Then all these breweries started opening, which gave tourists more reason to come here. It got worse when the tourists decided to not only visit here but move here too. That changed everything. The people who have lived here for their entire lives suddenly couldn't afford it. Real estate went up a lot and we couldn't afford houses anymore. We are getting pushed further and further out into the country and away from our actual homes. It's hard to watch our city being taken away from us," Jimmy said. "And the City Council thing. I know the guy running,

Ronnie Jenkins. We both were born and raised here so we have seen Asheville change a lot over the years. The changes haven't been for the better. No offense," he said, giving her a smile. He didn't want to offend her.

"No offense taken. I can understand your point. I didn't know things had gotten so bad here," she said.

"Like I said, Asheville didn't used to be like this. When we were growing up, there was very little downtown. No reason to go down there. Have you driven through there and seen the Fine Arts Theater?" he asked.

"I have, it looks like a nice place that shows independent movies I think," she lied.

"Well, that was a porn theater. As kids we liked it when our parents drove through there so we could see the posters hanging outside. That's just one example."

"You all want it to go back to that. Nothing downtown and porn theaters?" She asked.

"Of course not, the point we are trying to make is it's gone too far. We've gone from one extreme to another. All the people with big money moving in have driven the market so high that people who grew up here and have had family here for generations are being pushed out. Breweries are part of that. Needless pickle ball courts and new parks are another part of that. The two members of the City Council up for re-election have only lived here for a few years or something. What do they know about Asheville other than sitting on the front porch of the houses they overpaid for and staring at the mountains? I wouldn't be surprised if some of the politicians are corrupt. Oh crap, I've been talking for a while. I really need to get back to work or I'll be at it all night. Thanks for the coffee and conversation. I'll be back next week." Jimmy handed Susan his coffee cup and went to work outside.

"That was close," Ricky said, coming down the hallway. "I forgot he was coming today and next thing I knew he was out front. Great job getting him to talk."

"It was an interesting conversation. Did you notice how he lied about the warehouse? Then again, I didn't expect him to come out and tell me he was there. The thing is, after listening to him, I understand their point and don't totally disagree. I certainly don't agree with some of their tactics, like burning down a warehouse or organizing a boycott of local businesses," Susan said as they both went into the kitchen to brew more coffee.

"Yeah, I know, that's the hard part. Both sides have valid points. I'm starting to think our role will turn from investigating to mediating. We still have work to do to make sure we have all the information we need, and we need to keep in mind who is paying us."

Councilwoman Carnes and Councilman Bradley were huddled in the Mayor's office to discuss the tourism impact report. The rest of the Council agreed with the Mayor to let the two members seeking re-election be the face of the report, as well as the new park. That way if it went bad, it was on them, and the rest of the Council could distance themselves.

"I think we need to release this today and do a press conference, especially after the meeting on Tuesday night," the Mayor said. "Ronnie Jenkins shouldn't be a threat to your seats even after the other night, and I'm not sure Nick Zika has much of a following. They don't understand that the tourism dollars are saving Asheville from an economic depression."

"Exactly right," Councilmen Bradley said. "Before I moved up from Florida, we voted to build new parks and put a huge amount of money into tourism advertisements. Our goal was to have a park within two miles of everyone's house. I think we know more of what is needed here than anyone else."

"I agree, we saw similar stuff in Salinas. We relied on tourism as well. Sure, there are some growing pains, but it creates jobs and keeps the city moving forward. I don't understand what this group is upset about," Councilwoman Carnes said, ensuring she made her point in front of the Mayor. Although she got along with Councilmen Bradley, there was a sense of competition between them because they were elected at the same time.

"Let's meet back here for a final review at 3:00," the Mayor decided.

Jimmy pulled up to his next job, a little behind schedule because of his unexpected coffee break with Susan. As he arrived, he saw a WAVL news truck.

"Mr. O'Brien, we are from WAVL. Do you have time for a few questions?" Chris Marko asked.

"Questions, what do you want to ask me about?" Jimmy said.

"Your 'buckle up buttercup' speech the other night has gone viral. People are viewing the clip from all over the country and people all over town are talking about it nonstop. What do you think about that?"

"I think people need to take our government back. These people aren't representing us. Asheville is overrun right now. We need to get it under control. Asheville deserves better. Look at Ronnie Jenkins. He's a homegrown guy. Born and raised here, went to college close by and worked his way up at the bank. His family has been here for generations, and a lot of his relatives have been pushed out of town because of what they've done to this place. Ronnie is the guy you need to be talking to."

"But do you stand by what you said? That the locals or some group is going after Councilwoman Carnes's seat?"

"First of all, I'm not a politician so I mean what I say. To do something politicians don't do, I'll answer your question. Hell yes I stand by what I said. Yes, we are going after Councilwoman Carnes's seat or even the other outsider. Whoever wants to lose first, it doesn't matter to me. People who have lived here for all their lives deserve to be represented too." Jimmy was proud of himself.

"Thanks for your time, Mr. O'Brien," Chris Marko said.

Thinking he had nothing to lose, Jimmy yelled at the reporter as he walked away, "Hey one last thing. Is Darby Jones single? She's hot. Tell her I said hello."

"I'm not sure but I'll give her your message," he laughed.

Ronnie walked up to the microphone at the Asheville Downtown Business Owners Association luncheon. He looked out at the crowd that gathered for lunch and conversation with the City Council candidate. The association had a series of these luncheons with each of the candidates and today was Ronnie and Nick's turn.

"First, I want to thank you for having me here today, it is an honor to meet with you. I am Ronnie Jenkins and I'm running for Asheville City Council. But you may have heard about that on Tuesday night," Ronnie said. He got a small laugh from the hundred or so people gathered. "I have lived in Asheville my entire life and have seen it change a lot over the years. To be clear, I am not against tourism. I am against the reckless City Council policies that have let our city be overrun. Let's be honest, we can't have it both ways. The current City Council has spent massive amounts of money on advertising our city, or should I say their version of our city. They have offered tax incentives to bring in new hotels and restaurants. They changed traffic patterns, narrowed lanes on the busiest roads and at the same time we have seen a substantial increase in traffic over the last three years. This is what I'm against. What am I for? I want to take away the tax incentives. If someone wants to start a new restaurant or brewery here, or build a new hotel, I want them to pay their fair share. Why should we give them a break when it's our residents who need a break? I want to take an honest look at our infrastructure. When is the last time you heard the Council talk about infrastructure?" The applause grew louder with a few cheers mixed in. "I know I only have a few more minutes so I will leave you with this. I agree with my friend on Tuesday night. I'm coming for not only a seat on the City Council but also to take our city back. I will look out for the residents of our great city and not just look to increase city revenue. Save Asheville, vote for me, Ronnie Jenkins for Asheville City Council." Ronnie took a step back from the microphone and made eye contact with several people in the room as he got the loudest cheers yet.

As the lunch meeting broke up. Ronnie worked his way through the crowd shaking as many hands as he could. He was surprised but happy when several people not only gave him encouragement but also a check to help his campaign. As Ronnie walked out of the meeting, he passed Nick Zika who was walking in for his turn at the podium. He could feel the momentum shifting his way and he liked it. Nick stopped to talk and wish him luck before Ronnie left.

RJ wasn't invited to the luncheon, but he used the adage, if you look like and act like you belong, then people assume you belong. Sitting in the back of the room, RJ listened to Ronnie talk. His

main takeaway was that a lot had changed in the Jenkins campaign
since he saw him the week before. As Ronnie walked by, RJ
reached out, shook his hand and gave Ronnie a long look straight
into his eyes.

RJ and Ricky had decided that he would shadow Ronnie Jenkins
and keep an eye on his campaign. According to Ronnie's Save
Asheville campaign website, his next appearance would be at the
Council's press conference for the tourism economic impact
report. That wasn't scheduled to begin until 4:00. It was now 1:00,
so he had some time.

Near downtown was a taco shop that is a favorite among locals, so
RJ decided to have lunch and then check out one of the breweries.
Quack Taco is small, but they were using the space they had. He
was surprised at the menu choices, they all looked good. RJ settled
on a couple of beef bulgogi and a steak and cheese taco with a beer
to wash it down. He sat down, took a long pull on his beer, and
waited for his tacos.

As he ate, RJ thought about all that had gone on since he arrived in
town. He liked these pauses every so often so he could think. By
the time RJ finished his last taco, he agreed with Ricky that they
needed to figure out what was going on with the police as much as
the three locals and now one of their clients seemed to be mixed
up in it all too. He made a note to come back to this place before
leaving town, those tacos were crazy good. RJ headed to Asheville
Beer Facility, which was not far down the street.

RJ walked into the Asheville Beer Facility thought it looked like a
hiking convention had exploded. He hadn't seen this much flannel
and hiking boots in a very long time, and he lived in Nebraska
where it was already cold and snowy. RJ noticed immediately how
modern it was with all the concrete and steel. He liked the classic
rock they were playing, nothing like good music and hopefully
good beer. Not a lot of people were there so maybe the boycott
was having some effect. He ordered the IPA and liked it but liked
his 1554 better. Of the five or six people there, he guessed four
were tourists based on the way they were acting and the way the

bartender treated them. After a couple of beers, he left for the press conference.

The Councilmembers gathered in the Mayor's office for the final run-through before they were due outside. "Ok, the July festival generates $500,000 throughout the weekend. Another of our biggest money benefits for the city is the Christmas Jam Concert at around $3 million for the local Habitat for Humanity. We need to push that Warren Haynes is a hometown hero helping his community."

"Isn't it set up by the guitar player that founded Gov't Mule and played with the Allman Brothers?" Councilmen Bradley asked, showing his gap in local knowledge.

"That's him, but our biggest money generator is the breweries. The report shows they generate a billion dollars for the region. Remember there is more to the report, but these highlights should satisfy the media. Let's face it, the media will get the full study and report whatever they want. I've already reached out to WAVL to ensure we get good coverage," the Mayor said as she looked out her window, keeping an eye on her staff setting up the press conference.

"That's what's saving Asheville," Councilwoman Carnes said. "I don't see how restricting tourism, taking away tax incentives, and limiting building permits will save Asheville. Look at everything we have changed since we were elected."

At 4:00, just in time for the evening news, Ronnie watched as the two Councilmembers and the Mayor walked out of City Hall and up to the podium. Looking around, Ronnie guessed there were at least six media outlets there as well as a few people who happened to be passing by. The TV stations had their cameras set up and rolling. He looked across the crowd and saw Jimmy standing near the WAVL crew. Ronnie smiled because he knew Jimmy was disappointed that Darby Jones wasn't there.

The Mayor opened the press conference and introduced the two Council members. Although they stood side by side, Councilmen Bradley took the lead, making a comment about how great the weather was in our great city. Ronnie wanted to puke. He is terrible. Ronnie held his tongue until the right moment. This proved to be a good idea because as the press conference went on, more and more people gathered around.

"And that is the incredible economic impact tourism has had on Asheville over the last year. Are there any questions?" Councilwoman Carnes asked.

"Yes!" Ronnie yelled to ensure the media's microphones would pick him up. He moved closer to ensure he made the evening news. "How much of that money went to infrastructure or the homeless to address any of our city's issues?"

"Mr. Jenkins, I want to point out how great this is not only for Asheville but for our region. Hotels are booked to the max, restaurants and other local businesses are operating at peak capacity. This is a win for our great city," Councilwoman Carnes responded.

"Why don't you answer my actual question?" Ronnie yelled back.

"Or can't you answer it?" Jimmy jumped in. "Come on, answer an actual question for a change."

The Mayor could feel the event spiraling out of control and decided to step in. "Thanks everyone for coming out, we are proud of what we have done."

"Save Asheville! Vote for Ronnie Jenkins!" both Ronnie and Jimmy yelled toward whichever media microphone they could find.

"You two lost control quick. If you're not careful, one of you will be out of a job," the Mayor said.

RJ couldn't help but just stand there and laugh. Those two knew what they were doing. They made those two Council members look bad. He called Ricky to fill him in on his afternoon's adventure. Ricky was in the office watching all the feeds while Susan took a nap. RJ hung up after giving Ricky his update then started back to his car to call it a day. As he entered the parking garage, his phone rang. It was Ricky.

"Hey man, I'm picking something up on the scanner," Ricky said. "Police are going to four, no make that five businesses downtown because of protestors. We work for some of those places. Can you get to Asheville Beer Facility? I'm leaving now for Coxe Ave Brewery." Ricky grabbed his keys and put on his Red Sox hat. "Susan, we need you on the monitors, we have problems downtown," he yelled, closing the door.

"I was just at that brewery and am only a few minutes away. I'll give you updates as you're driving. I'll also get Susan on the line to give us police updates," RJ said. After RJ added Susan to the call, he got his earpiece in, pulled his Cornhusker hat down, and put on his sunglasses. He ensured everyone could hear him and went to work. "Ok everyone, welcome to the show. I'm RJ and will be your host for a short time." He could hear Ricky laugh and got a sleepy and cranky acknowledgement from Susan.

"I have roughly 20 people in front of the Asheville Beer Facility, all holding signs. Looks like they vary from 'Save Asheville' to 'Go Home Tourists' to "Down with Beer City.' I see a few that say, 'Rest in Peace Dave Finley.'" RJ looked for a good spot to observe the group. "I don't see anything that looks like they plan to do anything more than make a statement and disrupt business for a while."

Ricky looked for a parking space across the street from Coxe Ave Brewery. He found one almost in the same spot as he used the first day. "I have about 40 people with similar signs. I'm going to call Father Tim and see if he is in town and can help a bit," Ricky said as he got out of the car. He saw Brian Johnson standing in the window looking at the developing situation. Ricky gave him a wave to let him know he was there and noticed the sign in the window supporting Phil Bradley for Asheville City Council.

"No need to call Father Tim, he is standing beside me," RJ advised.

"Awesome, if it looks peaceful to you, ask him if he would stay there and keep an eye on that protest so you can check on Circus Act Brewery. It's closer to me but this one is larger and for some reason I don't have a good feeling," Ricky said, keeping an eye on three guys that had just walked up. They looked different than the others. They were the only ones with backpacks, and the packs looked a little too heavy.

"Got it. He is good, I brought him into the call. He will let us know if anything changes and he needs someone back over here," RJ replied.

"Welcome to the fun, Tim. Let us know if it starts to turn violent or you think it might," Ricky said as he moved to a better angle to see those three guys. 'Why are they wearing those knit caps? It's not that cool of a day for October. Are they just trying to look good or are they trying to hide in plain sight?' he thought to himself. "Susan put your snack down and let me know if you are keeping up with all this."

"How did you know I was having a snack? Anyway smartass, I'm a little confused about where everyone is. Can everyone repeat where they are so I can log it and mark the map?" Susan asked.

"Ok, I'm at the Coxe Ave Brewery and have about 45 or 50 people here. I am watching three of them closely. RJ, be ready to come back me up if this turns bad," Ricky said.

"This is RJ and I'm just getting to Circus Act Brewery. Not much happening here but I do have about 15 people with signs walking the sidewalk in front of the brewery," RJ said.

"Umm, this is Father Tim and I'm still at Asheville Beer Facility and it hasn't changed at all since RJ left."

"Thanks everyone. The police scanner seems to be saying what you all are seeing. They do have police at other businesses downtown, but it sounds like you are at the epicenter, Ricky. They are dispatching more police to Coxe Ave Brewery."

Ricky saw the other police cars coming down the road, bringing the total to four. Based on his gut feeling, he took pictures of the three guys that didn't fit in with the others. They weren't carrying signs, either. "RJ come to me. Something isn't right over here," Ricky said.

"Moving."

Ricky watched the three guys move through the crowd, which was now over 50 people. They blocked the door and the sidewalk. The police were monitoring the situation but keeping their distance. One of the three guys, wearing a brown flannel shirt and baggy blue jeans, took his backpack off his shoulder and Ricky saw him unzip it and reach inside.

"RJ where are you? I'm moving in, one of the three is up to something," Ricky said as he crossed the street.

"I'm walking up now and see you. I'm ready."

Ricky walked slowly to not bring attention to himself. The baggy jeans guy was in the middle of a crowd with his backpack on the ground. He reached into it to pull something out. Ricky came up beside him and waited. His friends were on opposite sides of the crowd.

"RJ, can you see the guy I'm standing beside?" he said while turning his back to baggy jeans guy so he couldn't hear him. "There are two other guys dressed just like him on the opposite sides of the crowd. No signs, baggy jeans, knit caps and backpacks. They don't fit."

"I see them."

"Keep an eye on them for me."

As Ricky turned back around, he saw baggy jeans guy reach for a brick. Ricky got up close to him and said, "I wouldn't do that if I were you."

The guy turned and looked at Ricky and said, "Don't worry about what I'm doing, old man."

"Put the brick back in the bag and walk away," Ricky responded more for RJ than the baggy jeans guy. Now RJ knew what they were up against.

"Screw you, this is for Dave Finley."

"I'm sure it is. Now, I'm only going to say this one more time. You have choices to make, I would choose wisely. Your first choice is to put that brick back in the bag and then put the bag of bricks down and walk away. Your other choice is you end up in a lot of pain. Like I said, it's up to you. Regardless of what you decide, I'm taking the bag of bricks and then I'm going inside to drink a beer," Ricky said.

RJ made his way towards one of the other guys and stood behind him. Brian Johnson was still standing at the window watching everything develop. He was keeping a close watch on Ricky Temple trying to figure out what was going on.

It was over in a matter of seconds. Ricky took a quick step to get in front of the guy and bent down like he was tying his shoe. Ricky came up smoothly with his fist to the guy's crotch and then his hand continued to his throat. With a firm grip on his throat, he left the guy gasping for air while his crotch was screaming in pain. As Ricky set him on the ground, he told him he should stay home next time and read a book or something because there are some great new local authors. Ricky grabbed the backpack and headed for the front door of the brewery. As Ricky got to the door, Brian Johnson let him in. Ricky walked to the back of the brewery and waited for Brian who was locking the door behind him. Ricky handed him the backpack full of bricks.

"Wait here and let me back in when I knock," Ricky said as he walked through the back door and back outside.

RJ walked up to the guy he was shadowing and leaned into his ear much like Ricky had just done. "Put the bag of bricks down and walk away."

"I don't know what you're talking about," was the response.

"That's ok. I know what I'm talking about," RJ said while giving him a cold stare. "Look into that crowd, you will see your partner on the ground. He's the one gasping for air, holding his balls and moaning in pain. You can look just like him if you want. Your call," RJ said.

A few seconds later RJ walked along the side of brewery carrying the backpack from guy number two. He turned to watch the guy walk to the other side of the crowd and meet up with the third partner. Guy number three looked very confused as Ricky came up behind him. RJ watched to make sure Ricky had no issues. This time it was very quick, and he just handed over the backpack and the two guys walked away from the protest, leaving their friend on the ground.

Ricky met RJ behind the brewery and got the bag RJ had taken from the second guy. "Go back out and keep an eye on the crowd while I talk to the owner," Ricky said as he knocked on the back door. The door opened and Ricky handed the two backpacks to Brian.

"Here are more souvenirs. I'll be out front until whatever this is calms down. But before I go back outside, we need to talk. I had a meeting with the other owners the other day and you weren't there," Ricky said while staring Brian directly in the eye.

"No, I was out trying to borrow supplies from other breweries to help out after the fire."

"Are you sure that is your story?" Ricky asked.

"It's not a story. It's the truth," Brian said becoming uncomfortable.

"Then explain this," Ricky said as he showed him the pictures RJ took.

"So, I had lunch with a friend. What are you accusing me of?" Brian asked.

Ricky then played a cleaned-up version of the recording of the lunch meeting. "Sounds to me like you are involved in some vote buying scheme."

Brian just stared at him.

"Are all three of you involved, or just you?" Ricky asked.

"It's just me. But I have gotten the others onboard with voting for Bradley as well as several other business owners downtown," Brian said.

"One of the people who is behind all the stuff happening at your breweries saw you. You are a big part of the reason for the warehouse being burned down. Are you going to tell the others? I hope you know that you are in way over your head," Ricky said.

"What happens how? Are you going to the police?" Brian asked. "You really don't have anything on me. Who's to say that he didn't borrow money from me and was paying me back."

"Yet you just admitted it to me when I asked if the others are involved," Ricky shot back. "If that's the way you want to play it. Ok for now," Ricky said as he walked out the back door.

"Everyone, we had three guys with backpacks full of bricks," Ricky said. "One of the guys was about to take one out and throw it at the front window. I was able to convince him not to do it. RJ took care of another one and I got the third. No issues on our end. RJ, if you would, head back over to Circus Act and see what's going on there. If it's quiet, have a beer and head for home. Tim, what do you have over there?"

"Over here, the crowd is down to a handful," Father Tim said.

"I also just had a talk with Brian Johnson. I'll fill you all in back at the house. Tim, do you have time to come over here? There's something we need to do," Ricky asked.

An hour later, Ricky walked up Coxe Avenue towards Pritchard Park. Sitting on a bench next to Father Tim was Lt. Dalton. "Right on time," Ricky thought as he crossed Patton Avenue to join them.

"What do you want, PI?" Dalton snapped. "I'm busy but came as a courtesy to Father Tim, your attorney?"

"It's private investigator. I wanted to give you pictures of three guys who were at the protest this evening who had backpacks full of bricks. One was about to throw one at the front window of Coxe Ave Brewery. I was able to persuade him not to," Ricky said while taking a seat on the next bench.

"Funny, the guy you persuaded to not throw a brick, looks just like a guy my cops found lying on the street in pain."

"That's a hell of a coincidence," Ricky said dryly.

"We know these three," Dalton continued. "They aren't anybody important. Local punks who are always looking for an opportunity to do something stupid. We'll bring them in anyway. Thanks for the pics."

"No problem. I'm here to help."

"Look Temple, tell me what you know. Why did you want me to come alone? I can tell something is going on. You don't think these three punks were involved in the warehouse fire, do you?"

"No, I'm positive they aren't involved in that. As for coming alone, let's just say I'm working on something and when the time is right, I'll hit you up again." Ricky stood up to leave.

"That's bullshit. Tell me what's happening. I'm not playing a game with some PI. You know I could bring you in for withholding evidence," Lt. Dalton seethed.

"No game, lieutenant. You know you aren't going to run me in, you probably know I'm closer to figuring this all out than you are. There might be something else going on that you might not be aware of. A brewery owner named Brian Johnson is up to something. He is getting cozy with the councilman running for reelection," Ricky said.

"Do you have anything I can use?" Dalton asked.

"I feel sure something is going on that you will need to know about, but we are just getting information on it. I need to make sure we have it right. I'm just asking for a day or so and you'll hear from me," Ricky said.

"Ok PI. I'll give you a little room to work."

Maybe you could run a license plate for me sometime. And it's private investigator," Ricky said, laughing as he headed for his car and home.

Chapter 12

"What a day we had yesterday, Asheville. Good morning, I'm Darby Jones. Our top story today is the economic impact report released by the City Council. Councilmembers Bradley and Carnes held a press conference talking up Asheville's economy and the effect that tourism has on it. They highlighted some of the top events the city sponsors. As you remember, City Council candidate Ronnie Jenkins and one of his supporters, Jimmy O'Brien, have been very vocal about their stance on tourism and what they say has a negative impact on our region. As the Councilmembers finished their remarks, Ronnie Jenkins shouted questions. The Councilmembers were not able to keep up with the barrage of questions coming from Mr. Jenkins and Mr. O'Brien. They abruptly ended the news conference as Mr. Jenkins and Mr. O'Brien continued to ask for answers. Earlier in the day, Ronnie Jenkins held a rally of his own. He had a very large turnout as he continued his stance that locals need more representation to save Asheville. With only a few weeks to go before election day, this looks like it will have a wild ending. As we reported last night, yesterday evening, rioters unexpectedly gathered downtown and targeted several businesses. The crowd numbers varied by location with the largest number, estimated at 60, blocking the entrance to Coxe Ave Brewery. They carried signs supporting Dave Finley, who you may remember was the local business owner killed by a drunk driver. Three of the rioters were arrested. WAVL has learned the three rioters arrested are the leaders of an organized gang that has been operating in Asheville. Coming up after a quick break, our reporter Chris Marko caught up with Jimmy O'Brien at one of his job sites. You may remember him as the guy who has gone viral for his 'buckle up buttercup' speech at the City Council meeting last week. You don't want to miss this. We'll be right back".

The Mayor stood up from behind her desk and glimpsed out the window of her office before walking over and turning off the news. She hesitated before turning around to start the discussion.

Before the Mayor could say anything, Councilmen Bradley vented, "I can't believe those guys. Yelling at us during our news conference. We were delivering great news for the city. His slogan that he wants to save Asheville doesn't even make sense. Growing the economy will save Asheville, using his language. Tourism will do that. Less tourism will hurt our economy. How does he not understand that? And why is WAVL using the word rioting? They were just protestors and calling those three kids the leaders of some group is pathetic. I talked to the police already about them and they are just some street punks. The media just made that up. They are not helping."

"You two blew it. Sorry, but it's true. You had a good story to tell, but you weren't ready for questions. Always expect something like that, especially during an election cycle. You lost control fast, too fast. Always have a prepared line to go back to, so you can deflect and keep moving forward," the Mayor said. "Jenkins's rallies are drawing more and more people. His campaign is resonating with voters. I know we need to keep growing the economy and tourism is what Asheville has to offer. He is trying to sell that tourism needs to be regulated, like they are trying to do in Hawaii. He thinks we can still have our quaint little mountain town. He doesn't understand that we can't go backwards. Your problem now is that people are listening to him, and he has sold a lot of people the idea that he is one of them and will be their voice. I plan to have a talk with WAVL about the three kids. If they want to continue to get the interviews and full access from us, they will need to play ball our way. One more thing for you two to think about, Nick Zika is gaining some momentum too. So, I wouldn't focus just on Jenkins."

The three politicians sat in silence for a few minutes. Each was trying to come up with an idea to take the momentum back. The Mayor couldn't help but think that, based on their poor performance at the press conference, at least one of them wouldn't be reelected.

"I think we team up with the police and do a press conference about the protests. I agree we need to get the media back under control. Show we support the local businesses and the police at the same time. You know, talk up the great work the police did in keeping it peaceful," Councilwoman Carnes said. "Maybe try to get a few of the owners up there with us."

"We need to be careful with that. I like the idea, but we don't want to make the protests out to be more than they were. They sure as hell weren't riots. Maybe we just issue a joint statement with the police department and use our backdoor channels to the media to get them to play it up for us," the Mayor said, glaring. She liked these two, but they were making it hard on her. "We write a joint statement praising the police, get some quotes from the two of you to be added in from our side. I'll call the Chief and see who he wants us to work with, most likely Lt. Dalton and the public affairs officer. When it's ready we will send it out through normal channels, but I'll call WAVL myself and rattle their cages a bit. We all need to be on the same page about what they are saying. I'll remind them they owe me." The Mayor had enough, and had other things to do. She sent the two Councilmembers to call the police department and write the statement.

"We have the momentum and need to keep the pressure on those two Councilmembers. Did you see the looks on their faces when the Mayor shut down the news conference?" Ronnie asked. "I'm going to do more rallies attacking the two of them until one of them breaks. Just this morning I got five more invitations to speak to groups and events. The best news is the campaign is getting a huge influx of donations so we can get more signs and maybe start looking at a TV ad."

Ronnie, Jimmy, and Billy had just finished watching the noon news while eating lunch at their favorite downtown taco spot. The problem was, they were so recognizable that people kept stopping by their table to offer encouragement as well as donations. Lunch took longer than expected.

"Ronnie, just to be clear, those protests downtown were not us. We didn't organize them or even hint at it. But I like it. People are starting to think and see what you are trying to do," Billy said, giving Ronnie a chance to eat while there was a lull in people stopping by. "I've seen those three guys they arrested. They were just kids. They've done it before." After taking a quick bite Billy kept going, "I'll put up your signs all over town. Today is a good day for it because I'll be in West Asheville and then in South Asheville again to do some estimates for pools for the spring. I'll do more on the way home too."

Jimmy sat there thinking and trying to run interference with supporters. Ronnie needed a chance to eat, but he also knew how important it was for Ronnie to shake hands. "Me too, Ronnie, I'll get some signs and put them out when I'm working this week. I know the press loves polls, any word yet on how you're doing now that the campaign is out there?"

"I'm still behind but gaining quick is what I'm being told. The big influx of money is going to help a lot and get me more attention."

"Well, hello boys. How are the tacos today?" Father Tim said as he walked into Quack Taco. It was another normal stop for him when he was downtown. "I've been seeing you guys on TV a lot lately. How do you feel about your campaign, Ronnie?"

"Father Tim, thanks for asking, I always enjoy visiting with you when you come to the bank. You know I wasn't getting anywhere until the Council meeting last week. The campaign is picking up steam. Not only are the polling numbers going up, but so are donations. Financials are way up and far exceeding what we thought we could do. When Dave was killed it really made me think about everything and gave me more of a purpose. You know we had been friends since kindergarten, so it is hitting all of us hard," Ronnie said. Talking about this made him have a flashback to Dave's memorial service, which made him emotional. Ronnie kept himself from crying because he knew it wouldn't be a good look. His campaign could do without someone with a cell phone, anxious to record a vulnerable moment.

Father Tim said, "I am sure you three are still grieving and will be for a long time. If any of you ever need someone to talk to please don't hesitate to call me." With that, Father Tim went and ordered his lunch.

"Guys, I gotta run. I'm due at my next speaking event. Thanks for all the help," Ronnie said. He headed to the door, giving a wave to Father Tim.

RJ, Susan, and Ricky sat around the fire pit, enjoying some fresh air, when Father Tim walked around the corner of the house. He took a seat and joined his three friends.

Ricky offered Father Tim a late afternoon cocktail.

"A beer would be great. I wanted to let you know that I was walking around downtown this afternoon and ran into Ronnie Jenkins, Jimmy O'Brien, and Billy Thompson. I asked about the campaign, trying to get a feel for what they are thinking and doing. He didn't say a lot but did say his polling numbers are going way up as well as donations. I thought that was an important bit of information."

"Thanks Tim," Ricky said, passing a beer over to him after refilling Susan's Chablis.

"What about me?" RJ asked.

"Get your own beer, jackass," Ricky shot back as they all laughed.

"One more thing," Father Tim said. "Ronnie brought up Dave Finley's death. He said it is a driving force behind his reinvigorated campaign. My phrasing. Not his. He started to break down talking about it but caught himself. I offered my help to them through the grieving process. I just wanted to make sure you all understand that when someone is in need, I will help them. However, I don't agree with the things they have done, like the warehouse fire. I do support you in your efforts to get a peaceful ending to all this. That's why I gave Clif and the guys your name."

"So much has been happening, we never talked about what happened when you confronted Johnson," RJ said.

"He denied everything. Tried to say he was just having lunch with him and that Bradley was repaying money he owed him," Ricky said. "Which is bullshit because I asked him if any of our other clients were involved, and he said no."

"Yeah, he was lying. I would say based on what I saw and heard as well as their mannerisms they didn't know each other well. It was awkward," RJ said.

"I tipped Dalton to it all as well but stopped short of telling him exactly what we are thinking. I wanted to talk to you first."

"I have no doubt they either were making or had made an agreement to exchange money for votes," RJ said definitively.

"That's good enough for me. Whenever the pace slows down, I'll get the info to Dalton. Let's make it his problem," Ricky said.

"Agree."

"But back to what you said, Father Tim, we don't want or need you to cross any lines. Just help us where you can and if you hear things that you think we need to know is all we are asking," Ricky said.

"Thanks for understanding that I'm walking a fine line here."

The two Councilmembers sat in the Mayor's office while she read a draft of the statement. She was getting more and more annoyed with these two. She was trying to help them keep their seats, but it was becoming a full-time job. The Mayor stood up and walked to her window that overlooked Pack Square Park. She couldn't help but notice the three homeless people lying on the benches wrapped in blankets. This reminded her of the homeless encampment she passed driving to City Hall each morning. She couldn't admit it, at least now, that she didn't disagree with what Ronnie Jenkins and Jimmy O'Brien had said. The homeless needed help, and the streets needed work. The purpose of having a solid economy was to use it to improve the city, not just to re-invest it in advertising to increase tourism. She knew that was for another day, though.

Nobody spoke. They waited to hear from the Mayor first. They all knew they were approaching the magic hour of 4:00 p.m. which is the deadline for getting news releases to the media before the evening news.

"And the police department approved this?" she asked.

"Yes," they said in unison.

Councilwoman Carnes continued, "The public affairs officer and Lt. Dalton provided their wording, and then we added what we wanted. We thought it would be a good idea to be confident because we don't think the actions the other day were appropriate. We mentioned the warehouse fire as an example of what is not good for the city. As you see, we ended with good news economic report to get that back out there and control the narrative."

"I called the WAVL General Manager, and he is ready to support. I also called Darby Jones directly, we know each other from events around town. She is ready to roll with it as well." The Mayor sat back down at her desk and looked at the clock on the wall. It was 3:45 p.m. She opened the email again and read the statement one more time before approving it. Finally, she looked up at the two of them and said, "Let's run with it. I'll send it to our public affairs team as well as the police department's team with my approval and ask for immediate release."

"We are starting tonight with news from the City Council concerning last weekend's events," Darby Jones said to open the first of three editions of the evening news. "The council just sent out a statement and here are some of the highlights:

The Asheville City Council and the Asheville Police Department are disappointed in the actions of some of our citizens in recent weeks. Although the Police Department does not have any leads, we ask anyone with any information about these events to call the hotline we have set up. The Downtown protests were not coordinated with the City or Police Department. As we approach the election, the City Council appreciates all your support and looks forward to continuing the progress this Council has made. Please do your part and think about the issues our city faces and do not be sidetracked by false narratives. We thank you in advance and as we like to say here, keep Asheville weird.

Thank you, Mayor, members of the City Council, and the Asheville Police Department for your guidance and leadership. You can read the statement in its entirety on the City Council's website as well as the WAVL website. We will be back after a short break with more news," Darby Jones said as they went to commercial.

"Ricky T!" Kenny King yelled as Ricky and his friends walked into Mitchell's. They decided to go out for dinner since it had been slow. "The usual all the way around?"

"Kenny, you're the man, set us up!" Ricky yelled back at their new friend.

They took their usual table and settled in for dinner and drinks. As their food arrived, they saw the news report on WAVL.

"Kenny, turn the TV up," Ricky said as the four of them gathered at the bar to hear what was being said. When the report was over, Ricky told Kenny to make their order to go and to put everything on his tab because they needed to leave.

When they got back to the house, three of them went straight to the living room to try and catch the news report again as they ate. Susan handed them each a drink and then went to the office.

"When you finish in there, you need to get back here. Our friends are talking about the news, and they don't sound happy," Susan said.

Billy, Jimmy, and Ronnie gathered in Billy's basement to discuss business. At first, they didn't think they had much to discuss, but then came the news. They were lucky Jimmy had turned it on to get a look at Darby, or they wouldn't have heard about the statement until later that night or maybe even the next morning.

Ronnie pulled up the Asheville City Council website and read over the full statement.

He read it to the group.

The Asheville City Council and the Asheville Police Department are disappointed in the actions of some of our citizens in recent weeks. The warehouse fire that destroyed the structure and its contents, which hurt several of our locally owned businesses, is unacceptable. Although the Police Department does not have any leads, we ask anyone with any information about these events to call the hotline we have set up. We are keeping the Mayor's office informed of our progress. Friday's downtown protests disrupted business and vehicle traffic. These protests were not coordinated with the City or Police Department. While the Police Department is working hard to continue to ensure the safety of our citizens, the City Council and city staff are working hard to ensure our great town remains prosperous. Actions like those of the last few weeks are not a positive look for our city and need to cease. The economic report released by the City Council shows Asheville is heading in the right direction. Slowing down economic growth will be detrimental to the city and entire region. We ask that you continue to work with us and not against us. The current Council members have a lot of experience in government, so please help us move Asheville forward. As we approach the election, the City Council appreciates all your support and looks forward to continuing the progress this Council has made. Please do your part and think about the issues our city faces and do not be sidetracked by false narratives. We thank you in advance and as we like to say here, keep Asheville weird.'

"So, citizens expressing their views is not good for Asheville or not good for those twos' reelection chances. This is bullshit!" Jimmy yelled. "Last Friday should have shown them that it isn't just our views, and we aren't making shit up. Lots of people are not happy with what they are doing. That statement is typical political garbage. They were probably too scared to have another news conference, so they are hiding behind a statement. And look how Darby praised it."

Billy paced around the room. He was thinking about grabbing a beer but was too mad. Ronnie just sat there, thinking.

"Could be they're scared. Maybe my campaign is scaring them because I'm gaining on them. Lots of people were talking about how they screwed up their own press conference. People are surprised they couldn't answer simple questions," Ronnie said.

"Do we need to escalate again?" Billy asked. He had grabbed a Busch Light but was still pacing. "They basically are saying they will win their seats and are the only ones who know how to run the city. They are going to continue what they are doing to our city."

Ronnie went to the Council's website and pulled up the statement again. He read it over to make sure he didn't miss anything and had read it correctly. Satisfied, he was ready to open the discussion. "If we escalate, what are we talking about doing?" he asked.

"We already burned down their warehouse. I don't think it did as much as we thought. Bobby said the word at the Police Department is they got supplies from the other breweries in town so they can keep brewing," Billy said, still pacing the room. "The protests didn't seem to have much effect, either. We could try another protest downtown but this time we could make it a full day takeover. Or we could go hardcore and go after one of the tap rooms like we did the warehouse."

"We could do both, or do we drop the information we have about Bradley?" Jimmy suggested. "Stop pacing, Billy, you're driving me crazy."

"I still think we hold the info on Bradley. We need to pick the right time, and we only have one shot at it. Billy, call Bobby and see if he would be able to cover for us again and then you two scout some of the tap rooms and see which ones are vulnerable," Ronnie said. "Which ones do you guys think we should scout?"

"Well, I think the logical one that needs to be hit is Coxe Ave Brewery since it has a connection to Dave's death. But maybe we shouldn't be logical. That might make it easier to trace back to us. I vote for the Asheville Beer Facility and Circus Act. I don't like their beer anyway. Who knows, maybe we should look at all three and decide later," Billy said.

"Ok, I hear you about Bradley. I just don't want to waste what we have. Billy is right, I think those three would be good to scout," Jimmy agreed.

"You guys scout them, and we will meet back here tomorrow night and talk it over. Make sure you call Bobby. I have another rally, so I need to get back downtown. I'll catch up with you guys tomorrow," Ronnie said as he walked toward the door.

"Holy crap, are they seriously considering burning down or bombing one of the taprooms?" Ricky said. "And why are they picking on our clients? We need to come up with a plan because this one we can stop if they are dumb enough to move forward."

Ricky looked at the map of downtown. "This is getting out of control. I think it's time to end all of this. I was hoping that the combination of the driver being charged, and Jenkins's polling going up, they would back off. The council isn't helping calm things down, though. They think they are, but it's just another misstep on their part. Susan, we will need you a bit more in the coming days if that's ok with you."

Susan was surprised because it was the first time he had asked her instead of directing her. "Well yeah, Ricky, you know I'll help anyway I can."

RJ, Susan, and Father Tim could feel the tension in the room. None of them had ever thought those three would take it this far.

"Father Tim, I think you will have a role in this, but I don't want you to feel uncomfortable. Like you said a little while ago, you are already walking a fine line. You need to let me know how much you want to know. You probably know more than you'd like about some of the things we have done as well as what they have done. Your call. RJ, I don't know how we have been so lucky but as far as we can tell nobody knows who you are or that we are working together. We need to get you home to Money and the farm. Your dad has his own farm to run. So yeah, it's time to finish this," Ricky told the group.

"I'm here until it's done," RJ said. "Do we bring the police in?"

"Not yet, I think I have an idea," Ricky said.

"Obviously I can't break the law, well I should say I won't do anything that breaks the law. But I want to hear your plan, so I'm

in and will let you know if it's something I can't be a part of,"
Father Tim said. "What do you have in mind?"

Ricky gathered everyone in the living room. The least they could do
was be comfortable while hashing out Ricky's idea. Susan went into
the kitchen to get snacks and water for everyone. She knew there
would be no more drinking until this was all over.

They were all seated when Ricky laid out his idea. "To start with,
somebody needs to be in that office all the time listening to the
bugs and watching where the vehicles are going. We will set a
rotation, Father Tim not included. The other two need to be ready
to drive a circuit downtown keeping an eye on our clients. I know
this has been said before, but every conversation in that basement,
every video from those cams, and all tracking on the cars needs to
be recorded and copied, then saved to multiple locations. I want
zero chance of losing any of our data. I think we will need it later.
Next, once we know where they are going to hit, we will converge
and stop it. This will be RJ and myself," Ricky said. "Susan, I have
a few research things for you." Ricky then took the next 20
minutes to talk everyone through the rest of his plan.

RJ thought the plan was good. Plus, he knew there would be
adjustments along the way. "I'll make up a rotation for the office
and post it in a couple of hours. I'll take the first shift since I'll
already be in there working on the schedule," RJ offered.

"From what you just laid out, I have no issues. I'll coordinate with
you, Ricky, as we get to my part," Father Tim said.

The next night, Billy, Ronnie, and Jimmy met up in Billy's
basement. They had been busy the last 24 hours.

"I talked with Bobby. He said depending on the plan and what we
want to do, he should be able to help. He also said the police still

don't have a clue about the warehouse or that he is helping us. Late last night I drove by a couple of the tap rooms we talked about. It was well after closing and they looked empty. A few lights on inside for security as usual," Billy reported.

"I saw the same thing," Jimmy said. "I'm not sure it will be as easy as the warehouse, but I think it's possible to pull off."

"I think you two should drive around the area during the day and walk around the area again after they close tomorrow. During the day look for businesses with security cameras facing the street. Notice where the streetlights are and how dark it is around the doors," Ronnie directed, asserting his role as the group leader. "You guys know, it's the same thing we did leading up to the warehouse fire. Go back tomorrow night around 10:30 and walk the streets. It won't be odd if someone sees you at that time of night. If it still looks good, we will set a date and start getting supplies. Then I think we should do another drive by the day before. As Jimmy likes to say, lets buckle up buttercups." They all laughed while they started mentally preparing for the next day and night.

"Ronnie Jenkins is not a dumb guy," Ricky said as they finished listening to the recording of the most recent planning session in Billy's basement. "RJ, you and I will be downtown tomorrow. When they start driving towards one of the breweries, Susan will let us know. We can't be far away so we can get some video of them driving around them. I'll take Coxe Ave Brewery and Circus Act if you will stick close to Asheville Beer Facility, RJ. The question is, do we appear at the tap rooms tomorrow night and persuade them to forget about lighting a fire, or do we wait to see if they move forward?"

"I think if we are going to end this, we start tomorrow night by stopping them as early in the process as we can," RJ said.

"I agree," said Susan.

"Ok, it's settled. We stop this crap tomorrow night. Tomorrow is going to be a long day, no need for anyone to be in the office all night. Susan, if you would, check all the recordings in the morning. RJ and I will meet to finish planning in the living room, and I'll let Father Tim know we are almost to his part." With that, they all went to bed to get ready for the next day.

Chapter 13

Susan was in the office doing research when Ricky got out of the shower. It was a stormy morning with heavy rain and winds. The weather was more like late September and not almost the end of October. Ricky looked outside and thought the weather was perfect for what Jimmy and Billy were doing today. RJ came into the living room and handed Ricky a cup of coffee.

"I went over everything that was recorded last night, but there was nothing important. Everyone was good and just stayed home," Susan reported as she walked down the hallway into the living room. "Nothing on the early morning news except for the traffic accidents near the construction on I-26 going out to the airport."

"That's ok, we won't be anywhere near there today," Ricky replied. "RJ, I think we should leave here as soon as soon as we finish talking to make sure we are down there ahead of them. Do you agree?"

"Yeah, that works. If they do what I think they are going to do, I want to get video of it. It won't prove much, but recordings of them driving very slowly by the breweries for no reason will be good for our case," RJ said as he finished off his coffee.

At 10:00 Susan called Ricky and RJ and told them Jimmy and Billy's vehicles were moving. Five minutes later, they were parked and standing at their assigned breweries waiting for Billy and Jimmy to come by. They communicated with Susan on the group call.

"Ricky, Billy Thompson is about to drive by Coxe Ave Brewery. He is coming down the street now," Susan reported.

"Ok, I see the Bronco, he is going very slow," Ricky said. He lifted his cell phone to video the car as it passed by. After the Bronco passed, Billy pulled into a parking lot and turned around to make another pass. "Here he comes again for pass number two."

"RJ, it looks like Jimmy O'Brien is coming your way now," Susan advised while keeping a close eye on her monitor.

"OK, I think I see his truck coming down the road." Like Ricky had done, RJ used his cell phone to take a video of Jimmy's truck driving slowly by the Asheville Beer Facility. Just as Billy had done, Jimmy found a parking lot down the street and turned around to pass by again before driving away.

"Guys, it looks like O'Brien is driving by Circus Act and they might be switching," Susan said. "Yes, O'Brien is now heading towards you, Ricky, and Thompson is driving over to where RJ is."

"Got it. RJ are you still over there? I'll sit tight until they are both out of the area," Ricky said.

"Yeah, I found a spot out of the rain so I'm good," RJ said.

Surprisingly, the two of them switched drive-by locations two more times. Ricky and RJ got it all on video to add to the collection. Susan let them know they were all clear and said they seemed to be heading for Billy's house. Ricky and RJ headed for their cars to go back to the house to see what they had in store.

As Ricky drove back to the house, he called Susan. "Ok, Susan we are up to your part. Make the call."

Jimmy beat Billy back to his house but was only a few minutes ahead of him. "I hate this rain but it's helping us. Not only did it give us a day off from work, but nobody was on the road this morning. Traffic was easy for a change," Jimmy said as they ran from their trucks to the basement door. "What do you think? Did you notice anything that will stop us?"

"Not really. I didn't see any cameras on any of the businesses pointing at the street. I know they must have been there, but I didn't see them. I think we should still go back tonight and walk by again. Let's take a closer look. Seeing the streetlamp coverage will be easier at night anyway," Billy said.

For the next hour, the two friends talked through their plan. They decided to target Coxe Ave Brewery and Asheville Beer Facility. Jimmy would do the Coxe Ave Brewery and that would leave Asheville Beer Facility for Billy. They would leave Billy's basement at 10:00 and plan to be back by 11:30. The only thing left to do was call Bobby Clark to let him know they would be walking around downtown tonight and ask him to keep an eye on them.

After listening to O'Brien's and Thompson's planning, Ricky and RJ decided they would leave the house at 9:45 to ensure they were in their spots before the two showed up.

"I made the call, so we are set for tomorrow morning. I also called Father Tim to let him know to be here early," Susan said.

Ricky and RJ spent the rest of the afternoon studying the downtown maps and coordinating with each other on where they would intercept Thompson and O'Brien. With plans made and escape routes determined, they laid down to get some rest to ensure they were ready for the night.

At 9:00, they assembled in the office for a final walk through. It was still raining but the wind was calming down a little. They spent the next 30 minutes going over it again. They hoped surprising these two and talking to them would be enough. Now it was time to do the job. As they sat in their respective cars, they did their final communication check and then drove off.

Jimmy found a parking space a couple of blocks away. He got out of his car and walked toward Hilliard Avenue which took him to Coxe Avenue.

At the same time Jimmy was walking up Coxe Avenue, Billy parked in a lot off Lexington Avenue. Billy walked across two parking lots which took him to Biltmore Avenue, just up the hill from the brewery. Billy went right to walk down the street towards Asheville Beer Facility. He walked slowly and looked around to take in as much information as possible without being obvious. As Billy came to the end of a building right before the brewery entrance, he felt an arm around his shoulder.

"Keep walking, shut up and listen. Forget your plans, you aren't scouting anything, and you can forget about any plans to set anything else on fire," RJ said firmly.

"But..." Billy said.

"I said don't say a word and I meant it," RJ said. "We know all about your plans and we are watching you. We know where you live, we know what cars you two drive. You're done."

Billy kept walking and went all the way down to the next major intersection. He had gone well past the tap room before he realized the guy was gone. He was stunned at what had just happened, so he got to his car as quickly as possible.

Ricky was not as nice as RJ. As Jimmy O'Brien walked up Coxe Avenue, Ricky slipped out from behind a tree just before he reached Coxe Ave Brewing. "Turn around and go home. You aren't checking out the brewery for cameras. If anything happens to this place or the other one you guys are looking at tonight, we are going to pay you a visit. Forget your plans, go home. No more fires. Do you understand, buttercup?" Ricky said.

"I don't know who you are, but you don't tell me what to do," Jimmy replied.

"You're right, you don't know who I am. That is the only thing you have going for you right now," Ricky said as he slipped away from Jimmy and into a shadow by a nearby store.

Jimmy went back to his truck and called Billy to tell him what had just happened. Billy said he had a similar thing happen to him and he had called Bobby to look in the area to find him.

"Call him back and tell him there are two of them," Jimmy ordered.

"Guys, I just heard on the scanner that a police car is going to drive by Asheville Beer Facility because he got a phone call reporting suspicious activity. RJ, if you are still in the area, watch out," Susan told the guys. She tensed up and moved to the edge of her chair.

"Copy, I see headlights coming my way. Could be a police car but won't be able to tell until it gets closer," RJ reported back to them. "It is a police car. Moving very slowly with his searchlight on all the buildings. He is looking for someone. I'm trying to get to the alley I saw on the map."

"Susan, we need to help RJ. Make the diversion phone call," Ricky ordered. "And quick."

"He's about a block away," RJ said, trying to stay in the shadows while looking for another way out.

"Asheville Police Department," said the voice on the other end of the phone.

"I don't know if this is an emergency, so I didn't call 911, but I just saw two men breaking into cars in the Asheville Tourists baseball stadium parking lot," Susan said, trying to sound scared and shaken up at the same time.

"Ma'am, can you tell me what you saw exactly?"

She sensed she needed to increase the urgency to make sure the police car didn't reach RJ. "Get someone here as fast as possible!" she yelled. "Now they are breaking windows." Click. After hanging up, Susan took the battery out of her burner phone and threw it away.

The police car continued and got close to where RJ was trying to hide. Suddenly, the police car's blue lights and siren came on and it sped off, rushing past RJ but going too fast to see him. Once RJ was sure the police car was far enough away, he went for his car.

"I think I'm good," RJ reported.

"Let's get home, we have an early morning tomorrow," Ricky said. He had been idling near RJ's location in case he needed to get his friend out of the area quickly.

Chapter 14

Early the next morning, Father Tim, Susan, and Ricky had coffee in the living room. RJ stayed in his room and out of sight for this part. The storm had passed, and it was a beautiful day. At 9:30, they heard Jimmy's truck pull into the driveway. Susan stood up, took a deep breath, and walked to the front door.

"Thanks for calling and giving me a heads up about the limbs down in the yard," Jimmy said to Susan as he jumped out of his truck.

"It's no problem. I knew you would be here in a couple of days anyway but thought it might be a good idea to get it taken care of," Susan said, looking Jimmy over. She thought he looked a little off, frazzled maybe. "Why don't you come in for some coffee before you get started?" she urged.

Jimmy didn't pick up on the tone from Susan and walked toward the front door. As he entered the house, he froze as he looked in the living room.

"What's going on here? Wait, you're that PI." Jimmy stuttered, trying hard to regain his composure.

"It's private investigator. Just have a seat, Jimmy. We need to talk," Ricky said.

"What is Father Tim doing here? What is this?"

"Jimmy, Ricky asked me to help find a solution to all the stuff going on around town. I think you need to sit down and listen to him," Father Tim said calmly.

"And you," Jimmy said, turning to Susan. "What's the deal here?"

"I know I told you my last name was Gilmore, but that is my maiden name. I'm Susan Temple, Ricky is my husband." Susan also spoke in a calm way to keep things from spiraling.

"Jimmy, you're focused on the wrong thing. Just sit down and let's talk," Ricky said again. "We know everything you guys have been up to. Father Tim has found a place for us all to sit down and talk it out and put an end to all of this."

Jimmy didn't acknowledge anyone. He just sat in a chair and stared out the window, trying to process what was happening.

"Listen Jimmy, we need you to get Ronnie, Billy, and yourself to Pigs BBQ, down by Asheville High School tomorrow morning at 9:30. The violence, protests, and boycotts need to end," Father Tim pleaded.

"Jimmy, it's time for us all to sit down and have a talk. This has gone far enough. To put the cards on the table, we can send the police what we have, and you guys will go to jail. The three of you have nothing to lose by being at Pigs BBQ tomorrow morning," Ricky said.

"I'll try, but can't guarantee anything," Jimmy said.

"To be honest, you don't have much of a choice. You guys will be there and that's all there is to it. If the three of you aren't there, we will go to the police at 9:35. You go to a meeting or go to jail tomorrow, your choice. I can't be blunter than that. By the way, did you get home ok last night?" Ricky took over because Father Tim's approach didn't seem to be working very well. Jimmy was in shock.

"That was you?" he yelled back at Ricky. "I should have taken a swing at you last night."

"That would not have gone well for you. Just be there in the morning. Look Jimmy, we've said what we need to say. It's up to you and your friends." Ricky and Susan stood up and walked into the kitchen, leaving Father Tim to walk Jimmy out, as they had planned.

Father Tim walked Jimmy to his truck and told him again to be there with the others in the morning. When Father Tim came back into the house, RJ joined the others, and they went over what had just happened.

"What do you think, Tim?"

"I'm not sure. He was still confused, adding this to last night's events. Hopefully he goes home and thinks this through. Most likely he is calling the guys to get them to meet up. If he does that, let's hope it's at Billy's," Father Tim said, looking out the kitchen window to the backyard.

They decided that vigilance was the most important thing for the rest of the day. Not sure what the Boys' reaction was going to be, they monitored all the feeds to get an idea. Ricky was most worried about Bobby Clark.

Jimmy frantically typed out a text. "Get to Billy's now!!!" Send.

Jimmy heard his phone ding as he received a reply. It was Billy. "On my way. What's up?"

He didn't want to explain it to Billy and then a second time to Ronnie. He was already driving to Billy's when Ronnie replied. "On my way. Finishing up a rally," Ronnie said. He pulled into the driveway at Billy's house. He didn't have to worry about getting in, Billy never locked the basement door.

Thirty minutes later, they were all gathered in Billy's basement. Jimmy took over the meeting and for the next 20 minutes walked them through all that he had learned earlier that morning.

"I told you guys last night that I had a guy tell me to go away as well. Whoever it was seemed to know everything. Hell, he even mentioned the warehouse fire," Billy said. Ronnie sat in his chair listening and trying to make sense of it.

"There's no way Temple could be at both places at the same time. So, he has help from someone. Father Tim?" Jimmy speculated.

"No, not Father Tim. That isn't the way he works," Ronnie said. "So, both of you were approached last night while you were scouting the locations. How did they know what time to be there, or that you were going at all?"

After a couple of hours of going over and over the information they knew, Ronnie and the boys still had very few answers. "And one last time, Father Tim told you directly that this guy was trying to end this once and for all, but if we weren't there tomorrow, they were going immediately to the police?" he asked.

"Yeah, that's what he said. They both kept saying this had gone far enough and it was time to settle it. He said we could go to a meeting or go to jail tomorrow," Jimmy said for the tenth time.

"The campaign is picking up speed and donations are flying in. I don't want to risk any of it. We don't know what they really know, and I think the only way to find out is to go to in the morning. I don't like it, though. Let's call Bobby to see if he can be in the area in case this goes badly. Also, ask him to drive by this house a few times tonight and see if he can figure anything out about our mystery fourth person," Ronnie concluded.

"Fourth person?" Billy asked.

"Yeah, we have Temple, the wife, Father Tim, and one more we don't know anything about. Could be the guy you two talked about from the Stein Mart parking lot a couple weeks ago. I say we go and see what happens."

Having finally come to an agreement, they decided to lay low the rest of day and get ready for what was to come in the morning.

Ricky ended his call that completed the next part of the plan. Now, late in the evening, Ricky, Susan, RJ, and Father Tim gathered in the office to keep an eye on the external security cameras. By 10:00

they had counted a police car driving slowly up and down the street four times. It never stopped, so they decided to set an audio alarm on the cameras to wake them up if anyone got near the house. Then it was time for some sleep.

Early the next morning, they sat in the living room having coffee and going over everyone's assignment for the day. As soon as Susan saw Billy and Jimmy leaving, RJ would go and retrieve their cameras and bugs then pick up Susan before making a quick stop on the way to the sit down. Father Tim would go with Ricky to their first meeting of the day and then meet the others at Pigs BBQ.

At 8:45, Ricky and Father Tim walked into Pritchard Park and were happy to see Lt. Dalton already sitting on the bench. As they walked up, Ricky took control. "We don't have long because we have another meeting to get to. You have a problem in the Police Department. One of your officers is helping the guys responsible for all this mess. My advice to you is to look at your records. See who was the first officer on the scene of the Dave Finley crash. Who was scheduled to be off and volunteered to work the night of the warehouse fire? Who was the only police car patrolling Riverside Drive? Which officer was going up down Graystone Road multiple times very slowly last night?"

"Why don't you just tell me," Dalton snapped back at Ricky. "Tell me what you know. No more games."

"One more thing, Dalton. I have something else for you regarding the Brian Johnson thing from the other day. I think it will help your career. By the time you get back to your office, there will be an envelope on your desk with some pictures and a copy of a recording. I think you will know what to do with it," Ricky said.

Lieutenant Dalton knew the meeting would go the way it did. Before he could call one of his detectives to follow Temple, his phone rang.

"This is Dalton."

"Hey Lieutenant, this is Detective Galloway. I was just driving through downtown and saw you meeting with someone in Pritchard Park."

"Yeah, what about it?" Lieutenant Dalton said.

"I was going by when your meeting broke up. I thought it was strange that a patrolman was in civilian clothes, following the guy you met with," the detective said.

"What? Are you sure? Which patrolman?" he asked.

"I'm positive. Officer Bobby Clark was in civies and was definitely following your guy. Do you need help with anything?" Detective Galloway asked.

It all started making sense to Lt. Dalton.

"No, I'll take care of this but thanks for the call," he said. He disconnected the call and dialed Police Headquarters. A few minutes later, Lt. Dalton hung up and put more pieces together before making two more calls.

Once Dalton had called Internal Affairs, he made his last call before going back to headquarters, "Dispatch, this is Lieutenant Dalton, contact Officer Clark and have him meet me in my office in 10 minutes. One more thing, did someone just come by and leave a large envelope for me?"

"Yes sir, some guy in a Nebraska Cornhuskers hat walked in and wanted to know where your desk was. We had someone escort him to your office and he left an envelope on your desk."

Ricky and Father Tim pulled into Pigs BBQ. They were the last to arrive. RJ and Susan stood in the parking lot waiting for them. "Well, their cars are here so that's a good sign," RJ said. RJ had just bent down and taken the car trackers off Billy Thompson's Bronco and Jimmy O'Brien's truck. With that done, the four of them walked to the front door.

They entered Pigs BBQ to the small area where customers order and pay. To the right is a room with tables and then beyond that is a second room with tables for customers to sit and eat. Susan went into the first room and set her laptops up on a table and sat down to wait. She wasn't sure she would need them but was ready just in case. Ricky got tea from the counter, thanked the owner for letting them use their restaurant, and walked to the back room. Ricky and Father Tim walked in and looked at everyone. He was a little surprised that everyone had shown up. RJ stood in the doorway to maintain control of the room if need be.

"I think we will talk about the most important thing first," Ricky said as he walked toward Billy and Jimmy. "Which one of you jumped me in the parking lot that first day?"

"Me and him," Billy said pointing at Jimmy.

"Who hit me in the back of my head and kicked me in the ribs?" Ricky asked more directly.

Susan heard someone scream in pain followed by the loud sound of a table crashing over. She peeked around the corner to see Billy Thompson on the floor holding his nose which had some blood trickling down as Ricky kicked him in his ribs

Ricky saw Jimmy pull his phone out of his pocket and start a text. "If you're texting Bobby Clark, I would forget it. There is a very good chance that he is now suspended from the police department pending an internal investigation," Ricky said, not knowing Bobby Clark had followed Lt. Dalton to their meeting and was spotted.

Ricky turned his back on Jimmy, walked toward the table, and took a sip of his tea before taking a seat.

"Let's get started. We have some ground to cover," Ricky said.

"Why the hell do we have to listen to you? I don't know who you are," Ronnie said as he stood up to leave. He was nervous and was having some regret about coming at all.

"Sit down, shut your mouth, and listen," RJ instructed him. "Good to see you again Billy," RJ said, winking at him.

"You're the guy from downtown the other night," Billy said, surprised.

"OK, look we have things to discuss. I know what you guys have been up to so here is what is going to happen. No more boycotts, no more protests, no more burning down warehouses, and no more planning to burn down a tap room."

"You don't know shit about anything," Ronnie snapped back, standing as if to leave again.

RJ looked at Ronnie and pointed at his seat. "I told you once to sit down and shut up. You really don't work and play well with others, do you?" RJ yelled at Ronnie.

Ricky turned toward RJ and mouthed the words, 'Don't work and play well with others,' trying to figure out where that came from. RJ just shrugged his shoulders as if to say, it just came out.

"Ronnie, to start with, a donation from all that campaign money you've raised should help to pay for the rebuilding of the warehouse you burned down. Why should they have to rely on insurance since you three are responsible for the damage? I know you are taking in a lot of money," Ricky said, winking at him.

"I think you're bluffing, you don't know anything," Ronnie said.

"Come with me, Ronnie. The rest of you just sit still. I will leave my partner to entertain you until we get back."

Ricky and Ronnie walked into the other room to the table where Susan sat. She put down her banana pudding as they approached.

"We have a non-believer. Give him the headset and play everything for him," Ricky told Susan.

Susan started with the recording of Jimmy and Billy from when they got home from setting the warehouse fire. When that was done, she showed the camera footage of them loading Sara Dunn's pickup truck with gas cans and the recording of the car trackers showing they were at the warehouse as it caught fire. Lastly, she played the conversation of the three of them discussing setting a tap room on fire. When the recordings were done, Susan went back to her banana pudding and sat quietly.

Ronnie sat there for several minutes. He looked shocked, so Ricky did not push him to go back to the others. Bobby had warned them the PI was going to be trouble. He never thought he would put listening devices in their homes or tracking devices on their cars.

Ronnie stood up and walked back into the other room. "Ok, we're listening," is all he said.

"What do you mean we're listening?" Jimmy shouted back at Ronnie.

"We were outplayed," Ronnie said. "Wait a minute. You said I will donate money from my campaign to rebuild the warehouse. I can't do that, that's campaign fraud."

"That's where your conscience kicks in, Ronnie? You burned down a warehouse, that's arson and in North Carolina that's at least a year in jail plus a fine. You planned the breaking and entering and vandalism of two breweries. Campaign fraud is where you draw the line? You boys need to take a long look at yourselves in the mirror," Ricky said.

"Don't preach to me," Ronnie yelled back.

"Someone needs to. You have been campaigning on how you are a better choice for your city. Do you even realize that if you get elected you will go into office as a crooked politician? You will always have to wonder when the police will knock on your door. You have created a strong following in this town. What do you think they will think when it comes out what the three of you have been up to?" Ricky snapped.

"THAT'S MY BUSINESS, NOT YOURS!"

"You made it my business when you attacked my clients. Do you want to do this on my terms, or yours?" Ricky asked.

"What do you mean?"

"I mean you could come clean yourself, drop out of the race and admit what's been going on. Show this town that you are the guy you have been pretending to be. Or I will arrange a meeting with Lt. Dalton and lay it all out for him. In other words, get some damn integrity and be the man you want to be."

"We need time to talk," Ronnie said. "One question. Why are you giving me a chance to come clean? Like you said, you can go to the police anytime you want. So why?"

"From one local boy to another, I want to give you the opportunity to do the right thing. I believe you have it in you. But don't think I won't call Dalton. This is a limited time offer. If I don't hear from you or see some sort of action in the next 48 hours, we will do it my way. The last thing I have to say is this. I have copies of everything I played for Ronnie. That's it, you three may go now." Ricky dismissed Ronnie and the Boys.

As Billy walked by RJ, he stared him down and said, "Next time I see you…"

"No, you won't. You aren't going to do anything. Keep walking," RJ said.

When Ronnie approached RJ, he stopped. "I know you from somewhere. Have we met?"

"We shook hands when you were leaving the downtown business owners meeting," RJ replied.

"I don't recognize you. Do you own a business downtown?" Ronnie asked.

"No," was RJ's blunt reply before walking over to join his friends.

As they walked out of Pigs BBQ, Ricky looked at the other side of the street and realized it was lunch time at the high school. Students were on the other side of the street waiting for traffic to clear so they could sneak across to eat. Ricky and Susan had three more people to talk to. He coordinated a meeting with Brian Johnson, for no reason other than he was the first one to answer his phone. Ricky told him he was heading to Circus Act Brewery and would be there in about 30 minutes to discuss the case.

Forty-five minutes later, Ricky and Susan Temple walked into Circus Act Brewery and saw a table in the corner with the three owners and a Miller High Life. "Sorry I'm late. I got stuck coming up the North Slope and had to wait in traffic to get to the South Slope. Thanks for meeting on such short notice."

"You do know there is no North Slope in Asheville, just the South Slope," Mike Lamb said.

"Look, I know that. When I was growing up here there was no South Slope either. Just my way of coming to terms with the way Asheville has changed."

At Ricky's suggestion, they all went to the office to talk in private. Ricky took a few minutes to explain the meeting they had just left. When he was done, Ricky asked Susan to play the recordings for their clients. They were paying him for the information, so they had a right to hear and see it all. They were surprised at the amount of data Ricky and his team had collected, legally or not.

"There is something else you guys need to know. I have been working with Phil Bradley to get him reelected," Brian said.

Ricky stayed silent. He wanted to see where this was going. He squeezed Susan's knee to get her attention and gave her a look asking her to follow his lead.

"We know, you have signs in your window, and you always tell us we should vote for him," Clif said.

"It's more than that. When I say I'm working to get him reelected, I mean he is paying me to get him votes," Brian replied.

"Gentleman, I learned of this a couple of days ago. I didn't say anything because I wanted Brian to tell you. The thing you need to know is the guys who vandalized your breweries, burned down the warehouse, and organized the stuff thrown at your windows know about this too," Ricky said.

"Do you have proof of that, Ricky?" Mike asked.

"I have some, and it was turned over to Lt. Dalton this morning."

Brian looked at Ricky but wasn't too surprised at what he had said.

"Brian, you need to leave now. We all worked together and supported each other, and you do this to us. Just get out of here," Clif said.

Brian stared at each person at the table. He stood up and walked out.

"I think we go to the police right now about the locals," Clif Jordan said.

"I'm asking you to give the three locals the 48 hours I gave them," Ricky said.

"What if they pack up and leave town?" Mike Lamb asked.

"I don't think they will. They are all from here, their families are all local. Where would they go? If they do, then we go to Lt. Dalton, and he will deal with it. As for Brian, I say let the police handle it. I talked to Lt. Dalton this morning and I'm sure he is on it. Let the system work," Ricky said.

After a few more minutes of discussion, the owners agreed to wait 48 hours. As Ricky and Susan left the meeting, Ricky turned to his clients and made a suggestion. 'Why don't you guys throw a fundraiser at each of your breweries to try and make up some of your losses?"

While Ricky and Susan walked to the car, they talked about what had just happened. "I'm a little surprised at what just went down," Ricky said.

"I wasn't expecting that to happen at all. It was a little tense, and I was afraid someone was going to take a swing at Johnson," Susan said.

"Fill the others in on this new development and I'll be back soon. I don't think this will take long."

Ricky dropped Susan off at the house. He had one more stop to make and he wanted to do it alone.

Ricky knew it was a long shot, but he wanted to try everything to make sure the problems ended. He parked his car, walked up to the front door, and rang the doorbell.

"Hi, you don't know me. My name is Ricky Temple. I'm a private investigator and you must be Sara Dunn," Ricky said when the door opened.

"I am but what does a PI want with me?" Sara said hesitantly.

"Can I come in so we can talk?" he asked.

They sat in the living room and Ricky imagined that a lot of grieving had taken place in this room since Dave Finley's death. He took a breath and started talking. "I was hired by a few owners of breweries downtown. I have a feeling you already know what I'm talking about."

"I have no idea what you are talking about," Sara said. As soon as he had said he was a PI, she knew exactly what it was about, but her loyalty was to her brother and friends.

"Ok. I just left a meeting with Ronnie Jenkins, Billy Thompson and Jimmy O'Brien. I know they are responsible for all the problems downtown. I'm giving them the opportunity to do the right thing and admit it themselves. If they don't, I'm going to the police. Ms. Dunn, I know they used your truck when they set the warehouse on fire."

"What does any of that have to do with me? Are you threatening me? Are you trying to say you are going turn me in if I don't do what you want?" Sara said.

"Absolutely not. I have no intention of ever telling anyone your truck was involved. I believe you have suffered enough. You lost your fiancé. Your brother is in trouble and so are your friends. All I am asking you to do is call Ronnie and tell him to do the right thing. That's it."

When Ricky said his peace, he thanked Sara, offered his condolences for Dave, and left.

The Boys went straight back to Billy's basement after the meeting with the PI. As soon as they walked in, they started tearing the place apart looking for bugs. Ronnie looked all around the recliners and the table between them. At the same time, Billy looked behind the bar. Jimmy took the front of the bar by Dave and Billy's chairs.

"They also had video of where we park and the door coming in here. Someone needs to look around for a camera," Ronnie instructed.

When Billy was done behind the bar, he went outside and started looking at the trees that are directly behind his house. After a few minutes he went back inside.

"I can see where something had been strapped to a couple of trees. Reminds me of the marks the strap for a trail cam makes. But there were no cameras out there," Billy reported.

"The only thing I found was a piece of tape under the front of the bar. It's sticky on both sides but no microphone," Jimmy said.

"After, what they showed me and you guys finding those things, it confirms they have been here," Ronnie said.

Now, Ronnie and the Boys were back to sitting in their usual seats in Billy's basement. The mood was gloomy, but they felt certain they could at least talk freely.

"I think we fight this. Call this Temple guy's bluff," Billy said. "Or I could take the fall for all of us. Ronnie, you have a good chance of winning. We need this. Dave would want that."

"He might have us. I don't know what to think. I'm not sure if you take the fall, it will clear us. Eventually they will get us all," Jimmy said to Billy.

Ronnie was listening to Billy and Jimmy when his phone rang, "Hey Sara. What's up?"

"A PI just left here. He said he met with you guys, and he has enough information to get you guys arrested. Ronnie, if it's true and he gave you a chance to save face, take it. Be the bigger man," Sara said.

"I can't believe he showed up at your house, too. We are sitting here talking it over. I think we all know what we need to do. Is it ok if we come pick you up in a few minutes?" Ronnie asked.

"Sure, are we going where I think we should go?"

"Yes," Ronnie said.

When he hung up, Ronnie let everything sink in and then turned to the others and relayed the phone conversation.

"The PI has too much on us. If he goes to the police, we are done. It might not be right away, but eventually they will be knocking on our doors. If they really do have Bobby then that could speed it up," Jimmy said.

"We were wrong," Ronnie said with his head hanging down. "One thing has stuck in my head from the coffee I had with Sara. She said, 'it's just wrong'. We let this all get out of control. The PI has us, so we need to do the right thing. When you step back and look at it, we started destroying the town that we said we were trying to save. No Billy, you aren't taking the fall for all this alone. I'm with you."

"Then it's decided," Jimmy said.

"I'm going to make some phone calls. If we are going to do this, I want everyone to hear it from me directly," Ronnie said.

When Ronnie was finished making his phone calls, it was time to do one more thing before his announcement the next morning.

Ronnie, Billy, and Jimmy left Billy's basement and got in Ronnie's 4Runner to drive the short distance to Sara Dunn's house. After picking her up, the four of them went to the cemetery to see Dave and explain everything to him. They all felt they owed him that much.

They stood around his grave, feeling the heaviness of the moment. "Dave, things got out of control," Ronnie said. After telling him everything that happened since his death, the three remaining Boys walked away to give Sara some time with him.

Chapter 15

Ricky, Susan, RJ, and Father Tim walked into Pappas Greek Table for dinner. They looked at the small sign at the entrance asking for support in the election for the owner, Nick Zika. While they waited for the young lady to came back to the hostess stand, Ricky's phone rang.

"Ricky Temple?"

"Yeah, this is Ricky T. Who's calling?" Ricky asked.

"This is Darby Jones from WAVL. Do you have a second?"

"Well, no I'm out to dinner with some friends, can this wait?" he said.

"No actually. I'm about to go on the air and wanted to know if you have any information about the news conference Ronnie Jenkins has called for tomorrow morning or about Brian Johnson being taken to the police department for questioning?"

"Why would I know about that? It sounds like you have me mixed up with somebody else."

"I have an anonymous source that says you have been involved with a lot of the things going on around town, ," Darby said.

"Who is this anonymous source?" he asked.

"I can't reveal my sources, you should know that," she responded.

"Darby, I'll be blunt. I don't believe in anonymous sources. When I hear anonymous sources, I think there is a 50-50 chance you are just making shit up. In other words, no source name, then no comment. Sorry but you have the wrong guy anyway, I'm in town with my wife and friend enjoying the nice clean mountain air," Ricky said. Click.

By the time he hung up the hostess was back to the stand.

"Yes, Mr. Temple we have been waiting for you."

"We need to stop in the bar to see the news. That was Darby Jones wanting a comment or information about what she is about to report," Ricky told the group.

"Good evening, Asheville. From the WAVL studios on Macon Avenue, I'm Darby Jones. We have two pieces of breaking news tonight. First, in an unexpected development in the City Council race, Ronnie Jenkins has called a news conference for tomorrow morning outside City Hall. Sources familiar with the situation tell us he is planning to drop out of the race. Second, Brian Johnson the owner of the Coxe Ave Brewery, was brought to the Asheville Police Department this evening for questioning regarding the election. As this develops, we will bring the latest to you. We will also be live tomorrow morning at the Ronnie Jenkins news conference. We learned a few minutes ago the owners of Asheville Beer Facility and Circus Act Brewing will be holding a series of fundraisers to help with the losses they have had recently. They have scheduled the first one for tomorrow night at Circus Act Brewery."

"Sounds like our three friends took our talk seriously and Lt. Dalton acted quickly on that information we gave him," RJ said as they continued toward the back of the restaurant.

The waitress came and asked what everyone wanted to drink. Before they could answer Ricky said, "Give them anything they want, it's on me." Susan gave him a kiss on the cheek as the others thanked him. They all knew it wasn't completely over, but RJ would be heading home in the morning after Ronnie's press conference. Ricky and Susan would go home soon, too. But tonight was for the team, and they all ate, drank, laughed, and were thankful they had a ride share, so nobody had to drive.

At 10:00 the next morning they gathered in the living room to see what Ronnie decided to do.

Ronnie Jenkins, Billy Thompson and Jimmy O'Brien stood together just outside the view of the cameras. They were nervous, scared, and in some ways relieved it was about to be over.

"Are you guys ready for this?" Ronnie asked.

Neither Billy nor Jimmy said anything, they simply nodded their heads. They all took a breath and looked out at the crowd that had gathered. Ronnie guessed there were at least a hundred people there. Once they were composed, they walked to the microphone together.

"Good morning and thank you for coming on short notice. I know there are a lot of rumors, so I want to say to start by saying that yes, I am withdrawing from the Asheville City Council race. Although I feel I have a lot to offer this city, the citizens of Asheville deserve better. The three of us are here to admit to you all that Billy, Jimmy, and I were responsible for some of the violence against the three downtown breweries. We are not proud of this in any way and decided we needed to admit our shortcomings to be better people and better citizens. We are responsible for the breaking and entering and vandalism as well as the warehouse fire a few weeks ago. Lastly, we helped plan the attacks downtown the same night as the warehouse fire. When Dave was killed, the three of us sunk to a new low. We didn't realize it at the time, but we let our grief get in the way of good judgment. There is no excuse for what we have done. We understand, a lot of you have placed your trust in me as a candidate and I ask that you now shift your vote to Nick Zika. I still feel it is very important to have a local citizen on the City Council. Lastly, before we go to the police department, we heard about the fundraiser at the breweries to assist with their losses. The three of us have pulled some money together and will donate to them. I ask anyone who was supporting me to attend tonight and donate. I know this is supposed to be a press conference, but we will not be taking questions. Thank you."

Neither Ronnie nor the others noticed Lt. Dalton and two police officers walking up behind them until he was done. He saw Sara Dunn standing in the back of the crowd and saw her smile at them. The three remaining Boys turned to Lt. Dalton indicating they were ready for whatever came next. As the police took out their handcuffs, Lt. Dalton could be heard over a live microphone telling his officers the cuffs wouldn't be needed.

The media cameras followed the small group as they walked from the front of City Hall to the police station.

With the press conference over, Ricky turned the TV off and turned to his friends who were all sitting in silence.

"I guess that puts this case to bed. I hate that it ended like this but I'm glad they took responsibility for their actions." Ricky said.

"Let's face it, they face several charges, but they are all respected businessmen who, as far as I know, don't have any records until now. That should help them. I have a feeling they will all be back if the citizens of Asheville let them and if they meant what they said," Father Tim said.

Ricky's phone rang. He looked at the caller ID to see it was Clif Jordan.

"Hey Clif, I guess you saw the news conference," Ricky said.

"We did. I'm here with Mike. Although we are happy that it's over, we still wish it had never happened. We want to make sure you are coming to the fundraiser tonight." Clif said.

"We are. Susan and I will be there with Father Tim, but RJ is about to head for home. I want to drop by later this afternoon and give you three a final report of what we did and how we got to this point."

"Sounds good. We'll see you around 2:00 at Asheville Brewing Facility if that works."

"We will be there," Ricky said. Click.

Ricky took a deep breath because now it was the hard part: saying goodbye to RJ. Susan gave him a hug goodbye as she wiped a tear from her eye. She knew how important he was to Ricky, which made him important to her. RJ told Father Tim if he ever needed anything to give him a call and then said goodbye to his new friend. Ricky gave RJ an envelope with his pay, which RJ immediately refused. Ricky told him he had more than earned it. Reluctantly, RJ accepted the check. With a final hug from Ricky, the garage door opened and for the first time in weeks, RJ backed his bright red Ford Raptor down the driveway.

Ricky gave one last yell to his brother in arms, "Call when you get there."

RJ laughed as he said, "Ok dad. Love you brother," and drove off.

At exactly 2:00, Ricky and Susan walked into Asheville Brewing Facility and saw their two remaining clients gathered at a table.

"Gentleman, I hope you remember Susan from our meeting a couple of days ago," Ricky said.

They all said hello to Susan and then the five of them walked to the office to get down to business.

Susan set up her laptop as Ricky walked the owners through everything they had done since he got to town. Ricky asked the owners if they wanted Susan to play the recordings again. They declined.

"Well, like we said before, that's a lot of information. We are both pissed off at Brian, we trusted him. It makes all of us look bad. What about the policeman who was helping them?" Mike Lamb asked.

"I pointed Lt. Dalton in the right direction about Bobby Clark. I've heard he has been pulled off patrol duty pending an investigation."

"Fair enough," Clif Jordan said. "Thanks for everything Ricky T. Father Tim was right about you. Make sure you come by tonight."

After their meeting Ricky and Susan went back to their rental house to get ready for the night. Around 7:00, Ricky and Susan walked into Circus Act Brewery. It was wall to wall people which was great for the plan to rebuild the warehouse. Ricky saw Livingston, the bartender he had met early in their investigation, pointing to the end of the bar.

"Watch this. Come with me," Ricky said, grabbing Susan's hand.

Ricky excused his way through the crowd and finally made it to the bar. Susan was surprised to see two seats with reserved signs on the back of them. There was a Miller High Life in front of one and a Chablis in front of the other.

"How did they know to do that?" Susan said. She didn't mind the good treatment but also thought Ricky didn't need anything else to inflate his ego.

"The first day I met with them I suggested they stock up on certain things," he told her.

A local band was performing, and the owners had placed empty barrels around the tap room for donations. Ricky, Susan, and Tim stayed for a while. When they were ready to leave, Ricky got the bill and paid it. As they walked out, he dropped a donation into one of the barrels.

The next morning, they decided to treat themselves and went back to the Grove Park Inn for coffee. Ricky hadn't had a cinnamon roll in a while and liked the one over there. On the way out the door, they saw the latest news report.

"Good morning, Asheville, I'm Chris Marko. We caught up with Councilmembers Bradley and Carnes and asked for their reaction to the Ronnie Jenkins news. They both said they applauded him for admitting what he had done and dropping out of the race. We asked for a comment from Phil Bradley about the reports he has been implicated in dealings with local business owner Brian Johnson. He had no comment on 'speculation and false reports' and they added that they both were looking forward to their next term in office."

The next morning, Ricky and Susan loaded the Ford Escape. It was time to go home, but first they would have a farewell lunch with Father Tim at Mitchell's Sports Bar.

"Kenny, you're the man," Ricky said as they walked to their usual table.

"Ricky T. The man. I'll get you guys the usual."

Sitting in the dark corner that had become another home, the three old friends talked about all that had happened.

"You know, listening to everyone over these last few weeks, I don't know what to think. Bradley and Carnes thought they were saving Asheville, I know that they didn't use those words but it's what they meant, by having increased tourism to bolster the economy. They were creating jobs through the hospitality industry to support the huge influx of tourism." Ricky was partially talking to his wife and friend but mostly was just talking out loud. "Then you have Ronnie and his Boys who said they wanted to save Asheville by restricting tourism and trying to get that small mountain town of old back. They want to get rid of tax incentives and make people pay to come in here, hoping some would be reluctant. I don't know."

"You know, thinking about this, after sitting at the Sunset Terrace, sitting in the patio of the rental house, and driving around looking at all these incredible views, I wonder," Ricky said, pausing for a second. "Did Asheville ever really need saving by anyone or was it just greed?" Ricky just let that hang there. It felt senseless to him.

After lunch, Ricky gave Father Tim an envelope like the one he had given RJ. After Tim thanked him, Ricky took a second envelope from his pocket and handed it to Father Tim. He told him, "This one is for your Parrish."

Father Tim looked at the checks and said, "You know it's strange, a couple of times a year the Parrish gets anonymous donations on checks just like these, but there is never a name on them, and this bank is not in our area."

Ricky winked at his lifelong friend as they stood up to say their goodbyes. Susan gave Father Tim a long hug and stepped out of the way so Ricky could do the same. Just as they were about to walk away, the door to Mitchell's opened and in came a petite blond walking very quickly toward them.

"Mr. Temple, I'm…"

"Darby Jones the queen of anonymous sources," Ricky said cutting her off. "How's business? What's your agenda today?"

"You really don't like me, do you?" she asked.

"It's not you. It's the media in general. It's drifted so far from what it used to be. You don't have any interest in facts, you want to pick a few facts that fit your agenda. That is a big disservice to the country," Ricky said.

"I think you are naïve, Mr. Temple," Darby said.

"That may be true but at some point, the American people will demand better. You will have to decide for yourself which side you are on. So maybe instead of a story about me or trying to get information from me, you should interview Father Tim. The holiday season is coming, and he has a lot of programs to support his Parrish and community that could use some publicity." Then he winked at Father Tim as he and Susan walked toward the door.

Ricky turned to Susan and said, "Shall we?"

Susan slipped her arm into his and said, "We shall."

"Kenny, we are leaving. The short blond over there will be paying for our lunch today. Here is a check for the rest of our bill, make sure you give yourself a good tip," Ricky said.

"You got it, Ricky T. We'll see you next time you're in town," Kenny said.

When they got to the car, Ricky opened the door for Susan and then walked around to the driver's side and got in the Escape.

They pulled out of the parking lot and made their way to the highway. As they got onto the entry ramp, Ricky turned on the 80's channel on satellite radio. Just as he did, a very familiar song was starting.

"Hell yeah, this is an 80's classic!" Ricky yelled. "'I Melt with You' by Modern English." As he merged with traffic, Ricky was singing off key, Susan was seat dancing, and Asheville was getting smaller and smaller in the rearview mirror.

Epilogue
Two Weeks Later

Ricky tried to sleep in, but it was election day. He loved election day and knew he would be up late watching the results. It was 9:30 when Susan got home to their condo on the north side of High Point. She walked in carrying two large coffees, a cinnamon roll, and a chocolate croissant. She handed Ricky his coffee, proudly showing her 'I Voted' sticker on her shirt.

"How long was the line today?" Ricky asked.

"It was short, since it was storming out. That rain is coming down hard out there. Are you planning on staying up to watch the results again this year?" Susan asked.

"I am. The funny thing is, the only race I'm curious about is the one up in Asheville. I wonder what will happen with Ronnie Jenkins out of the picture. He had a big following when he dropped out."

"I know. I want to hear about that one too," Susan said.

"I got a call from Father Tim. WAVL reported this morning that Bobby Clark was fired from the police department and the DA is looking into potential charges. It's sad. Of all people, a police officer should know better than to get involved in that stuff, and he could have stopped it. But the biggest news is Phil Bradley was arrested by the FBI and North Carolina Board of Election Investigators for election tampering when he walked up to vote. They picked up Brian Johnson at his brewery as he was closing it up for good. Now that's poetic justice," Ricky said.

"That's great news. Hopefully Sara Dunn is ok. She lost her fiancée and now her brother is in trouble," Susan said.

"While we are sitting here, do you want to go over the France trip?" Ricky asked.

"Sure. The flights are booked for the middle of March, I can't remember the exact date. We go into Paris and stay there for a week."

"Right. Isn't it the fourth day we go to Normandy to see the landing beaches?"

"Yes, that's right and I'm working on the museum tickets and tours we talked about. I'm excited. I know you have always wanted to go to Normandy, and after going to Pearl Harbor I want to see it too," she said.

"Then we fly back here? Any new jobs on the horizon for you?" Ricky asked.

"Yes, we fly back here and no I don't have any new jobs lined up."

"I was thinking, why don't we go down to Sully's Irish Pub after we eat and watch the results there for a while? We really haven't been out much since we got back," Ricky suggested.

"I like it. I was going to make some fried chicken for dinner. It's election day and there isn't anything much more American than fried chicken."

At 7:30 Ricky and Susan drove the short 10 minutes to Sully's Irish Pub in downtown High Point. Ricky parked in a lot across the street. They waited in the rain for some cars to pass and then crossed the street and walked into the pub. Ricky was happy to hear Flogging Molly being played as well as seeing Riley Simms behind the bar.

They waved to Riley as they walked to their usual seats.

"Here's your Chablis, Susan. Ricky, do you want your usual?" Riley asked as she put a Sam Adams Boston Lager and Powers Gold Irish Whiskey in front of him.

"Will you guys ever serve Miller High Life here? It's the champagne of beers you know," Ricky said.

"No, we won't. We have this discussion almost every time you come in here," Riley said with a smile. They were all friends and she and Ricky always picked on each other.

"What's your WIFI password?" Ricky asked as he watched Susan pull her tablet out of her bag.

"You know we don't have WIFI. Johnny wants everyone to talk to each other instead of staring at their phones all the time," Riley said.

"You do have WIFI because you are streaming music. Look, we just want to pull up a TV station in Asheville to see the election results up there," he said.

"Ok. It's Prohibition1933," she whispered so nobody else would hear.

"Where is good ol' Johnny Sullivan anyway?" Ricky asked. Johnny Sullivan, the owner, is a friend of Ricky and Susan.

"He left early and mad. Tommy and Gina Bonetti were in here drunk and raising hell. When they left, he decided to get out of here. He went to go vote and then to the parks and recreation department to do something about next season's coed softball team," Riley said.

"Tommy and Gina Bonetti? The ones who own Tommy's Tire Emporium?" Ricky asked.

"Yeah, they really don't like each other that much. Sometimes they come in here to piss Johnny off."

"Ok, I remember now," Ricky said.

"I think we should be seeing some results soon. It's 8:00," Susan said as she made her way to the WAVL website.

Ricky's phone rang and he saw it was RJ. "Hey brother. What's happening?"

"I'm watching the Asheville stuff online so I thought I would call," RJ said.

"Hold on. I'll dial Father Tim in, and we will have the team back together," Ricky said.

After a few seconds, he got Father Tim on the line with everyone. Ricky turned on his speakerphone.

"Ok, here we all are. Susan is with me, and we are all online waiting to see what Darby has for us," Ricky said.

"Here we go," Susan said.

Everyone was waiting for Darby Jones. Then they heard it. "In the Asheville City Council results, we have two seats available. In order of finish the results are Bobbi Carnes with 25,909 votes; Ronnie Jenkins with 24,813 votes; Nick Zika with 22,952; and in distant fourth place is Phil Bradley with 9,392 votes. One surprise is the 1,300 votes Jimmy O'Brien got as a write in candidate. Since Ronnie Jenkins dropped out of the race due to legal issues, the two seats will go to Bobbi Carnes and Nick Zika."

"Well, Ronnie and his boys got what they wanted, just not the way they wanted it. They have a local on City Council and a brewery out of business," Father Tim said.

"We did our part. We saw the dark side of Beer City that most people don't see. I think the results are what they should be," Ricky said.

"That's about the best Ronnie was going to do, considering the circumstances," RJ said.

"Ok guys. Thanks again for everything. Until the next time," Ricky said. Click.

Susan's Chablis was empty, and she asked for another. As Riley refilled Susan's glass, Susan got a phone call and stepped away. Ricky looked over at her. Susan smiled at him, reminding him how much he loves her smile. When she was done with her call she walked back to Ricky.

"That was the lady I worked with at the Naval Academy Museum right before you retired. She wanted to see if I was available to do some work in the spring. A few Academy grads are donating quite a few artifacts, and they want me to come up and help. She said it would take a maximum of two weeks. They are targeting late March," Susan said.

Ricky took out his phone and looked at his calendar. "That's perfect. The Red Sox have opening day in Baltimore this year. I say we change our flights home from France to go to Baltimore instead of Greensboro. We'll spend whatever time you need in Annapolis, then go to opening day and come home."

"Sounds like a plan to me," Susan said.

The next morning, Ricky and Susan drove the 40 minutes south to her cousin's lake house on High Rock Lake. They do this often, especially when they need a quick break and don't have the time to go to their Outer Banks house. For early November it was still warm enough to sit on the dock and enjoy the view. The wind was brisk, and they could tell winter was coming.

After drinking coffee and enjoying the lake view, Susan turned to Ricky and said, "I'm hungry and now my hair looks like shit."